Alice in Nurseryland

AF471851

The Annotated Alice in Nurseryland

Lewis Carroll's newly discovered suppressed precursor to *The Nursery "Alice"*

Introduction and Annotations by

Byron W. Sewell

evertype
2016

Published by Evertype, 73 Woodgrove, Portlaoise, R32 ENP6, Ireland.
www.evertype.com.

This edition © 2016 Michael Everson.
Text and illustrations © 2016 Byron W. Sewell.

Byron W. Sewell has asserted his right under the Copyright, Designs and Patents Act, 1988, to be identified as the author and illustrator of this work.

All rights reserved. No part of this publication may be reproduced, stored in a retrieval system, or transmitted, in any form or by any means, electronic, mechanical, photocopying, recording, or otherwise, without the prior permission in writing of the Publisher, or as expressly permitted by law, or under terms agreed with the appropriate reprographics rights organization.

A catalogue record for this book is available from the British Library.

ISBN-10 1-78201-152-8
ISBN-13 978-1-78201-152-1

Typeset in De Vinne Text, Mona Lisa, ENGRAVERS' ROMAN, and Liberty by Michael Everson.

Illustrations: Byron W. Sewell.

Cover: Michael Everson.

Printed by LightningSource.

Introduction

For about the last five decades, every new edition of *Alice's Adventures in Wonderland* has included an apparently obligatory introductory essay explaining, among other things, that the *real* name of the author was not Lewis Carroll, but actually Charles Lutwidge Dodgson. Frankly, this is no longer a well-kept secret.

However, this isn't to say that it wasn't a deep secret for a *very* long time. My wife, Victoria, owns a copy of the sixth edition of *Alice's Adventures in Wonderland* with an 1869 owner's inscription, followed by a note indicating that the owner didn't find out about Lewis Carroll's true identity until 1884![1]

And, as hard as it is to believe, a little noticed 1986 survey by *International Teen Person Magazine*,[2] revealed that 65 percent of the world's teenage population currently believe that Lewis Carroll is a pseudonym of Walt Disney.

As sad as this is, that's not the worst of it. Most of those who *do* know who wrote the *Alice* books don't have a clue that in 1880 Charles ("Charlie")[3] Lutwidge ("The Dodo")[4] Dodgson decided to

[1] Formerly in the collection of the late Denis Crutch.

[2] May 1986, pp. 16-17. A photocopy of a photocopy, provided by alert alligator collector Alison Tannenbaum of Chelmsford, Massachusetts. Reprinted in the Appendix, without the publisher's permission. since the magazine has discontinued publication and the former owners couldn't be located.

[3] His beloved mother's term of endearment. Dodgson refused all but his closest

capitalize on the great success of *Alice's Adventures in Wonderland* by producing a highly abbreviated version of the story, in his own quaint words (and strange capitalization), "to be read by Children aged Nought to Five."[5]

It is obvious from the suppressed edition, which is the subject of this book, that Dodgson's real motive in producing the abbreviated version was to meet young girls by approaching their mother's with a complimentary copy.[6] Once ingratiated, one thing would lead to another, and before you could recite Jabberwocky in Urdu. The Do-do and "Gurdy" Thomson[7] would be sketching the little girl "undraped", as they quaintly put it.

The same *International Teen Person Magazine* survey cited above estimated that only 0.001 percent of the people alive in the English-speaking world have ever heard that *The Nursery "Alice"* was ever published. Let's face it; it's never been a big seller,[8] in

friends permission to call him by this nickname. According to one unsubstantiated "legend", one hapless child-friend, who made the mistake of addressing him as "Uncle Charlie" was suddenly sent packing.

4 "Do-Do-Dodgson", as he stammeringly referred to himself in *Alice's Adventures in Wonderland.* This isn't a very deep literary secret either. You could call him a Dodo, but didn't dare call him Charlie! Odd.

5 "Preface" to *The Nursery' "Alice,"* London: Macmillan, 1889. It is doubtful that very many children "aged Nought" actually managed to read it, especially with words like "Storkling" and "Bantam-Cock", to say nothing of "Hippopotamus". Evidently the educational system was much further advanced in Victorian England than it is in present-day Canada.

6 Dr Phalen Greenpody has made much of this. See his monumental work, *A Jungian Approach to Erotic Children's Literature,* Boston: Higgledy-Piggledy Books, 1953, Vol. VI, pp. 12,756-13,843.

7 E. Gertrude Thomson, illustrator of *The Three Sunsets and Other Poems (1898),* used designs of naked fairies to illustrate Dodgson's book based, no doubt, upon sketches of nude children (quite possibly child-friends acquired with the help of complimentary copies of *The Nursery "Alice"*).

8 The original print run of 10,000 sets of sheets was rejected by Dodgson in a fit of "pickiness" as being too brightly coloured, perhaps not realizing that most children like bright colours. Four thousand of these sets were flogged to the tasteless Americans. He had another 10,000 sets of sheets printed in more civilized colours (this extravagance by a man who didn't want to spend the money to burn a candle at night), which were to be sold in England, to English

spite of its pretty coloured pictures.[9] What is even less well known (estimated at no more than $1.4 \times 10^{-8}\%$ of the world's entire population, English-speaking or not)[10] is that the published version was not what Dodgson had originally envisioned.

The literary world has apparently ignored the stunning revelation in the "Letters to the Editor" section of *The Edmonton Journal* for 6 June 1942, which stated:

> Dear Editor: I have inherited the personal papers (largely for seed catalogues and tractor repairs) of a long-time Alberta resident and barley farmer, who was a distant cousin[11] of the Rev. Robinson Duckworth, renowned friend and colleague of

children with more refined sensibilities. The remaining garishly coloured sheets were used in later cheap editions, which presumably only appealed to the English lower classes (probably American immigrants). A chromatic comparison of the colours for both printings has concluded "there isn't really all that much difference between the two." Some medical opinion exists that Dodgson may have simply been suffering a migraine on the day that he rejected the first printing, and that *everything* probably looked very bright to him. Fewer than two hundred copies of *The Nursery "Alice"* are known to have survived The Blitz and WWII paper drives (copies were pulped for paper for maps). Over half of these surviving copies are in the private collection of Dr Selwyn Goodacre, who by coincidence lives in Derbyshire, just down the lane from where Annie Thorlackson lived for many years. See Note 19. Typical selling prices listed on Bibliofind range from USD 500–2,000 for ordinary copies, depending upon condition. Inscribed copies to child-friends (most of which are actually forged) demand USD 8,000–10,000. Don't you wish that your own great-grandmother had been a child-friend in 1889?

9 Since Dodgson supervised the colouring, the illustrations prove conclusively that Alice wore a golden yellow dress (with a large blue bow), a white apron trimmed in blue, blue stocking, and a blue bow in her hair. Most subsequent illustrators of the *Alice* books have gotten it practically all wrong. The reason is probably because they (like most of the rest of the world's population) had never heard of the existence of *The Nursery "Alice"*. (Evertype is one publisher which gets it right.)

10 One person in seven billion (the estimated population of the entire world)—that is, something probably known only by the author of this present work.

11 Probably Heinz Zager, late of Sylvan Lake, Alberta (a wide spot in the prairie, just west of Prentiss).

> Charles Dodgson, better known as Lewis Carroll, author of the world's most famous children's story, *Alice's Adventures in Wonderland.* Included in these papers is a manuscript of a suppressed abbreviated version of this classic, entitled *Alice in Nurseryland.* This curious work is illustrated with a series of "happy-faced" characters intended for very young readers. I would be willing to trade the manuscript and some associated letters for salvaged tractor and combine parts. —Jerome Beaver, Prentiss, Alberta.

I recently acquired this manuscript in a garage sale in beautiful Dead Deer, Alberta.[12] Included with the manuscript was a collection of revealing letters between Robinson ("Ducky") Duckworth and his mother:[13]

> Ch. Ch.
> July 1, 1880
>
> Dearest Mum,
>
> I write to tell you of yet another interesting evening with Charlie. He has hit upon the idea of publishing an abbreviated version of his *Alice* book for the nursery. He showed me the manuscript, on which he has spent many a sleepless night (you no doubt recall his dreadful insomnia).[14] He has entitled "The

12 Saturday morning, 25 March 2000 at the residence of Kim Powers, Dead Deer. Alberta (a rural farming town just east of Sylvan Lake), priced at CAD 14.00, but negotiated down substantially. ☺

13 Sadly, the postage stamps had been removed from all of the envelopes. Why do people insist on doing this! ☹ Robinson Duckworth's mother was Mrs Duckworth.

14 Tormented by bad thoughts (and presumably even worse dreams), Dodgson was ironically both afraid *and* unable to go to sleep when he wanted or needed to. Some estimates are that he often got less than one hour of sleep per night, probably explaining how he managed to get so much done in such a short lifetime. In his own words, "many who have known what it is to be haunted by some worrying subject of thought, which no effort of will is able to banish … there are mental troubles, much worse than mere worrying, … skeptical thoughts, … blasphemous thoughts, unholy thoughts, which torture, with their hateful presence." As if that wasn't enough, he even refers to "that 'unclean spirit' of the parable, who brought back with him seven others more

Thing" (for I can not but refer to it as anything else), *Alice in Nurseryland.* It took me the entire evening to convince him that the project as presently envisioned "needs a heck of a lot of work".

For the illustrations, he has invented something which he calls "happy faces."[15] These are little more than plane geometric figures, such as circles and triangles (Charlie is ever the mathematician) with two oval eyes, and a line for a mouth. Some of them look basically like this: ☺ As much as I hate to admit it, these faces are strangely appealing, though I forbear to tell him lest he become encouraged and proceed with this hideous project. He has even come upon the idea of colouring these faces in pretty colours: it quite takes one's breath away to see them. Alice's face is as yellow as a canary and she looks like she has hepatitis. The Cheshire-Cat's face is purple, and the poor thing looks like it's been poisoned with strychnine. The wretched Duchess is pea-green and looks like she's been struck with cholera or food poisoning (too much pepper in the soup, perhaps?). The Queen of Hearts has a face as red as blood, and one has the impression that she will momentarily suffer a coronary thrombosis.[16] And

wicked than himself." There is no evidence that he was thinking of girls, in spite of what Dr Greenpody has claimed. Dodgson authored his classic (though little read) book on recreational mathematics, *Curiosa Mathematica Part II: Pillow Problems* [1895] ("all problems solved in the head while lying awake in bed at night") in response to this condition. He did indeed have a *lot* of problems with his pillows. There is some medical opinion that he suffered from allergies (which caused his migraines) as a result of mites and their faecal droppings. Had he but changed his sheets and pillowcases more often, and thrown out the pillows every six months or so, he would likely have slept much better.

15 It is not well known that the modem world credits the creation of what has become known as the "Smiley-Face"™ to Harvey Ball of Worcester. Massachusetts, who designed it in 1963 to cheer up the depressed employees of an insurance company. There is no evidence that Harvey had ever seen Dodgson's manuscript of *Alice in Nurseryland.* Franklin Loufrani secretly registered Ball's design in 1971, unknown to Ball for almost thirty years, and he has made millions off of someone else's idea. This reminds one of the American piracies of the *Alice* books. Ball is understandably very unhappy. ☹

16 As Martin Gardner (see *The Annotated Alice)* and many others have noted, *Alice's Adventures in Wonderland* clearly demonstrates Dodgson's fondness

this for children in the nursery! This seems more a nightmare than a curious dream!

He has intentionally written the story in such a sugary, condescending style as to be quite nauseating to a normal adult reader, though I must admit that it might well appeal to mothers whose brains have temporarily turned to pudding by the rigours of childbirth. He intends to carry copies of The Thing with him on train journeys and seaside holidays as gifts for little girls in hopes of thereby making their acquaintance.

He seemed quite distraught at my decidedly negative reaction his efforts. So, I convinced him to have the published Tenniel illustrations[17] enlarged (almost everyone loves these as much as they love the story itself), and have either Gurdy or (better yet) Tenniel colour them so that they would appeal to small children. He has reluctantly agreed that this would be a better plan.

We then had a lengthy discussion about the appropriate colours for Alice's costume. For some reason Charlie seems intent on making her look like she's wearing the Swedish flag. I tried to convince him to use a simple blue dress and plain white apron, but he would have none of it, insisting that only a tasteless American would dress her up like that.[18] He is probably right.

In order to be sure that he doesn't relapse and publish the "happy-face" version I have paid him 30 shillings (which I can ill-afford!) for the manuscript and illustrations. I intend to burn

for death jokes, and his choice of colours for *Alice in Nurseryland* as indicators for potentially fatal diseases, was likely the result of this "sick" vein of humour. He was also very fond of "Knock, Knock" jokes, as evidenced by their repeated appearances in *Alice in Nurseryland.* The famous missing pages from his diaries are thought by some Carroll experts to have recorded some of his favourites, and that they were burned by the Executors of his estate in an attempt to hide this low form of humour from the world. One of his favourite jokes goes like this: "Knock! Knock!", "Who's there?", "Alison.", "Alison, who?", "Alison Wonderland!" See Alan Tannenbaum's best-selling book, *1,001 Alison Jokes,* Dead Deer: Storkling Press, 1993.

17 As is well known, Duckworth reviewed the original manuscript of *Alice* and convinced Dodgson to solicit Tenniel to do the famous original illustrations. The world owes him a great debt.

18 Once again, Dodgson's words have proved eerily prophetic (shades of stereo-isomers and inedible Looking-Glass milk), as evidenced by the pervasive image of Alice perpetrated by Walt Disney (1951).

them at the next expedient opportunity. I feel it to be my Christian and English duty.

Please give my best regards to Cousin Annie when she visits you in a fortnight. I have enclosed a specially bound copy of Charlie's comic poem, *The Hunting of the Snark,* as her wedding present. Please give it to her with my best regards for a happy marriage to Reginald (have you ever noticed that he bears a striking resemblance to Hank's "Broker"?). One can only hope that Reginald will meet a Boojum before the fateful wedding day[19] and spare Annie his indignities!

Your loving son,
Ducky

Washing-on-Lyne, Derbyshire
July 10, 1880

Dear Ducky,

Please don't bum Charlie's happy-faces until I have a chance to see them. There's a dear! I will give Annie your present. It's a lovely book and I'm sure that it will bring her much happiness. Reginald's not such a bad sort, when you get to know him a little better. And he *is* frightfully rich, which is what really matters to her, after all.

XXX + OOO
Mum

Ch. Ch.
July 18, 1880

Dearest Mum,

I will bring The Thing with me when I come for holiday next month. We can use it to build a fire to toast cheese after you have seen it.

Love,
Ducky

---

19 Reginald H. Thorlakson. Even though the marriage occurred on schedule, it was sadly never consummated, and there were no children. Annie Thorlakson never bothered to have the marriage annulled and went on to brief fame as the inventor of the potato masher, which along with the invention of the potato peeler, has done much to alleviate the drudgery of the average housewife whose husband is fond of potatoes. It has been estimated that the combined worldwide sales of the potato masher have exceeded CAD 10 billion since its invention, though Annie personally made less than five pounds on the idea.

Washing-on-Lyne, Derbyshire
August 2, 1880

Dear Ducky,

I write with news that Annie's Reginald is horribly murdered—blown to teeny tiny bits by a bomb at his favourite pub, The Snark and Bathing Machine—on the night of their wedding! Only a cad would have abandoned his new bride at home for a quick pint with the lads before setting off on his honeymoon. She's better off without him! You've had your wish come true, certainly. The Snark was a Boojum! Annie can't bear to read Charlie's book now, and has sold it to a secondhand book dealer for a farthing. I thought she should have gotten more for it (she could hardly have gotten less!), seeing as how it had such a lovely dark blue and gilt binding, and was inscribed by Charlie with such a clever acrostic poem.[20] Who knows? Charlie might be *really* famous someday and it might be worth something in a hundred years or so.[21] Still, I can't blame the poor dear for wanting rid of it.

Your Father and I are looking forward to your holiday: he is repairing the fishing tackle. There won't be a pike or a trout in the district that's safe when you two set out for them.

Our horrid neighbours steadfastly refuse to pay for the repairs to my cucumber frame. They have even filed a suit against us for

---

20 Surely one of the funniest nonsense poems ever penned, a rival to "*Jabberwocky*". The first and second-to-last letters of the verse repetitively spell out ALISON WONDERLAND, something *very* difficult to do (try it yourself for a few verses, if you don't believe it!). The Dodgson Estate has refused my repeated requests to publish the poem in this volume. I can only say that it involves a walrus, a talking fish, a lost safety pin. and a very cute little girl in a bathing machine. You will have to use your own imagination until the Lewis Carroll Society finally publishes the poem in a forthcoming issue of *The Carrollian.*

21 Her copy of *The Hunting of the Snark* was auctioned at Sotheby's in 1992 for GBP 8000, then a record for the book, and is now in the collection of Dr Selwyn Goodacre, who at last count owned at least 301 different printings of the classic nonsense poem, including a complete run of all 85 of the Macmillan English and American editions, the beautiful little yellow Mervyn Peake things, and translations into 42 different languages, including the very rare Urdu and Gujarati editions. Dr Goodacre has informed me that he is not particularly fond of "Knock, Knock" jokes [private correspondence].

the wrongful death of their prized cat! As if it was our fault that their monster was chasing a poor robin on our property. As Charlie's Duchess would say, "There's a moral in that—'The best defence is a good offence'."

☺

Mum

As can be seen from her closing, Robinson Duckworth's mother was quite smitten with the original manuscript for *Alice in Nurseryland* and rescued it from Duckworth's fiery furnace.

Ch. Ch.
February 20, 1889

Dearest Mum,

Charlie has been hard at work these past two months finishing the text for his new abbreviated version of *Alice's Adventures in Wonderland*, which he has sadly re-titled *The Nursery "Alice"*. I liked his first title better. It is still as sweet as treacle and just as condescending, but thank goodness he has abandoned his "happy-faces" and taken my advice to have some of the original illustrations coloured by Tenniel himself. The new version will no doubt appeal to certain classes and should sell well enough at the projected selling price of four shillings.

Charlie mentioned that he is considering having some jewelry, such as cuff links and watch fobs, fashioned in the likeness of his original "happy faces." I shudder to think that this hideous thing might yet be foisted onto an unsuspecting world. I advised him to consider the American market, where they would no doubt sell like "cold bottled beer in the desert". The former colonists simply have no taste in such things![22]

Your loving son,
Ducky

[22] The yellow happy-face watch fob made its first appearance in Boston in 1893. The only surviving example is held in The Smithsonian, where it is on permanent display, alongside the oldest known piece of unchewed Double-Bubble chewing gum (in the original wrapper) and the earliest known book of paper matches (advertising The Mouseling Bar and Grill on 42nd Street, New York City).

The entire manuscript is presented following this introduction, with all of it's warts and imperfections. It was evidently written in the dark, using the contraption that Dodgson invented[23] to allow him to do this, thus avoiding the extravagance of having a candle burning all night; evidently a penny was *really* worth something in Victorian times. The manuscript is barely legible and it took a team of three graphologists two months to decipher it. Because of this, I have elected not to reproduce it in facsimile. Instead, I have faithfully transcribed it, as if it had been typeset, using the format for the published *Nursery "Alice"* as a template. This is how it might have looked had Duckworth not talked him out of publishing it.

Dodgson only got around to water-colouring a few of his illustrations, and these are included in facsimile. However, the text clearly describes the colours he intended for many of them, so the reader can readily imagine what they might have looked like. The colours have faded over the years, and one must again rely on his or her imagination as to what they would have looked like when first painted.

The manuscript contains numerous emendations, some of which are enlightening. I have included some of these within <angle brackets> so that it is possible to see how the work was composed and edited.

A line-by-line comparison of the manuscript with the published version reveals that Dodgson did a major rewrite of most sections for the published version, reverting to a simple retelling of the famous story. In most cases, the final version is decidedly better in the sense that it is more suitable for distribution to the general public rather than as a personal presentation in hopes of gaining yet another child-friend for his personal collection. Thus, it is

23 Basically a board to be held in your lap so that you can write in the dark. Dodgson had high hopes for the invention, but it had essentially zero appeal, since normal people don't like to stay up all night writing in the dark. However, this idea did eventually contribute to the concept of the modern computer keyboard, which is essentially an electronic version of his original idea. Oddly, the entire manuscript was written in dark green ink, not the characteristic purple or black that everyone (including forgers) associates with Dodgson.

reasonable to assume that lots of little girls wound up with copies of the published version whether they were cute and/or clever or not.

And, certainly, the final coloured Tenniel illustrations are vastly more appealing than the happy-faces Dodgson originally planned (though, in my judgement, not nearly so funny). It will be up to you, the Reader, to make the final assessment as to which version you like best. Your conclusion might well depend upon whether you are English, with refined sensibilities and impeccable taste, or a tasteless, filthy-rich and crass American, who will buy almost anything (bright colours, smudged printing, characters with goofy eyeballs, coloured faces, pirated editions, etc.). If you are a Canadian then you can go either way, having been influenced (and contaminated) by both cultures. It's great to be a Canadian, eh?

Byron W. Sewell

"—a plump little damsel … whose pale round face lit up for a moment with a half-smile …"

—Her Radiancy

A Tangled Tale (1885)

Lewis Carroll

"Lies, lies! Mendacity and lies!"

—Big Daddy

Cat on a Hot Tin Roof (1958)

Tennessee Williams

Alice in Nurseryland[24]

[24] The original manuscript has a series of potential titles stricken through. These include: *Alison Wonderland*, *Alice in the Nursery*, and *The Nursery "Alice"*. Obviously, Dodgson came back to this last title for the published edition, though there is a consensus that he made a poor choice. The best choice would have been *Alison Wonderland,* and it's a crying shame that he didn't take it.

A Happy Face[25]

A happy face:
Safe refuge from a stranger's glare,
From heavy burdens, life unfair,
And rudeness everywhere!
She how she encircles us in gaiety—
In joyous mirth and pleasantry!
Smile on then, happy golden disc,
And grant us yet another kiss.

A happy face:
Little love-gift from a darling child,
Instant brightness whene'er you've smiled.
Shine on then, happy golden face,
On each of us bestow your grace, .
Nothing else could take your place![26]

<Demons and tormenting sprites!>[27]

---

25 There is general agreement that the poetry here is inferior to that published in *The Nursery "Alice"*.

26 The second verse is an acrostic, with the first letter of each line spelling the name ALISON.

27 It is uncertain if this line was intended to be part of a third verse acrostic of WONDERLAND, thus completing Dodgson's favourite joke. Perhaps he was

Preface.[28]

(ADDRESSED TO ANY MOTHER).[29]

Please accept this book with my sincere compliments: It is intended to be read by Children aged Nought to Five.

I couldn't help but notice that your young Daughter is very Beautiful and quite Clever. Would it be all right if I: a) Take her to the theatre the next time you are in London?; b) Escort her to

just having one of his typical bad nights, and was recording what he saw or felt, and it has nothing to do with a third verse. The prefatory poem for *The Nursery "Alice"* has only two verses, so the latter possibility is probably the correct one.

28 Dr Selwyn Goodacre, the world's leading expert on Dodgson's peculiar use of punctuation marks, has written extensively in various issues of *Jabberwocky* about why Dodgson chose to end the titles of the various sections and chapters of *The Nursery "Alice"* (as he does here) with a full stop. Conventional grammar uses a full stop to end a sentence, not a fragment or a title. In Dodgson's defence. Dr Goodacre has quoted Humpty Dumpty from *Through the Looking-Glass,* Chapter VI: "When I use a word … it means just what I choose it to mean—neither more nor less." Dodgson obviously took the same position in the use of full stop (and other marks as well).

29 Well, actually addressed to any mother with a very attractive, prepubescent daughter.

the studio of my Famous Artist friend, Gertrude Thomson, to <sketch her *sans habilement*>[30] pose undraped as God intended, for sketches? (I can assure you that I have no intention of taking *any* photographs, but if any are taken I will see that you get the negatives); c) Play with her on the beach on your next seaside holiday to Eastbourne? d) Teach her Symbolic Logic?

Thank you so *very* much indeed! Your Famous friend,

Lewis Carroll
Easter-tide 1890

Character references available on request.

30 French for "in your birthday suit".

Contents[31]

---

31 Many critics who are able to count have noticed that the number of chapters in *The Nursery "Alice"* is different from *Alice's Adventures in Wonderland,* which has twelve.

32 This is essentially the only difference in the Contents from the final published version in *The Nursery "Alice"*. Dodgson likely changed it back to The Pig-Baby so that he might sell a few more books (to those mothers unlucky enough to have a horrid little boy).

Chapter I.

The White Rabbit.

One afternoon Alice was on a picnic with her sister, who was reading her a very boring story.[33] Alice wasn't happy so she decided to go to sleep. She had a very curious dream.

Would you like to hear what it was that she dreamed about? I'll tell you in a minute. Do you ever have bad dreams? You do? Me, too! That's why I try to stay awake as long as I possibly can. If I try *very* hard I can stay awake for sixty hours straight. You're

[33] Probably either "Novelty and Romancement", "The New Belfry at Christ Church" or "*Eight or Nine Wise Words about Letter Writing*".

probably wondering how I can manage to do this.[34] Well, I'll tell you my secret. I do it by standing up at my desk. Have you ever noticed that it's hard to sleep standing up? Of course this sometimes makes me *very* grumpy, especially around grown-ups. Some of them think that I'm *neurotic.*[35] If they had dreams like *mine* they would want to stay awake, too! Well, this is what happened in Alice's dream.

Suddenly a fluffy White Rabbit ran by. Alice jumped up and ran after it, a big grin on her little round yellow face once again. If you look at the picture you can see what she looks like. Her face is yellow because she has a sunny disposition, not because she is from the Orient.

[34] According to Karl Shaw in *The Mammoth Book of Tasteless Lists* (London: Robinson, 1998), Frederick the Great of Prussia once "drank up to 40 cups of coffee a day for several weeks in an experiment to see if it was possible to exist without sleep. It took his stomach three years to recover." Shaw also notes that "Honoré de Balzac died of caffeine poisoning; he regularly drank about 50 cups of black coffee per day."

[35] In Martin Gardner's memorable words in the Introduction to *The Annotated Alice* (New York: Potter, 1960, p. 9): "The point here is not that Carroll was neurotic (we all know he was).

The White Rabbit checked his pocket watch, then said, "Oh dear, oh dear! I shall be too late! The Duchess will be so angry if I've kept her waiting!" Why do you think he was worried? Well, because the Duchess was a very cross old lady![36] And the White Rabbit

[36] Judging from Tenniel's illustration, many readers have suggested that it is much more likely that both the Duchess and the Cook are men in drag. Dr Greenpody has made much of this. See *A Jungian Approach to Erotic Children's Literature,* Vol. VIII, pp. 18,120–18,241. Sir John Tenniel was reportedly a great fan of vaudeville, and this was likely at least partly the

knew she might even be angry enough to cut off his head and have her Cook invite him to join them for dinner.[37] Do you like to eat rabbit? You don't? Neither do I!

With that, the White Rabbit popped down a hole and Alice dived right in after him. You shouldn't do this, by the way. This is only okay to do in a dream. Alice laughed and laughed as she fell. "This is as much fun as bathing naked on the beach!" she declared. <Do you like to do that, too? I'd like to, but I'm too old now. If I did I might well wind up sitting next to the King's Messenger.>[38]

After a long fall she landed on a pillow[39] that <made a funny noise>[40] someone had thoughtfully placed there to catch little girls and she wasn't hurt a bit! Don't you wish that

inspiration for his illustration.

[37] This is the first of many death jokes, of which Dodgson was so fond.

[38] *Through the Looking-Glass,* Chapter V. "He's in prison now, being punished."

[39] At least *Alice* doesn't seem to be having any pillow problems.

[40] Dodgson has here foreseen the invention of the whoopee cushion (1953). He was well aware of vulcanization, of course, which had been discovered in 1846 and made the invention of the whoopee cushion possible. Whether he would have found it funny is a different matter. Probably not.

someone would always place a pillow right where you are about to fall down?

She looked up and saw the White Rabbit running away. Its silly hop made her laugh all the harder as she chased after it.

And so, that was the beginning of Alice's curious dream. Do you ever have dreams of being a famous model and posing for an artist <to sketch your lovely body>?[41] Or traveling to London to see a play?[42] Why not pester your Mommy to let you do that sometime? As you grow older you will find that if you pester your parents about something long enough

[41] According to Martin Gardner, in the Introduction to *The Annotated Alice,* p. 11: "He thought the naked bodies of little girls (unlike the bodies of boys) extremely beautiful."

[42] Dodgson loved the theatre and went to see a show in London at every opportunity. It will probably come as no surprise that his favourite play was Savile Clarke's *Alice in Wonderland,* which he apparently saw at least 83 times after its opening on Christmas 1886 at the Prince of Wales Theatre in London. His next most favourite play was *Tusker!*, a comedy about a young girl who befriends a Walrus she encounters on the shingle on the Isle of Wight and hides him in a bathing machine from marauding Eskimos intent on harvesting his unusually long tusks. The play was inspired by Sir Alfred, Lord Tennyson's epic poem, *Maud.* Dodgson was not a great fan of vaudeville, however. He would often purchase a ticket for a seat up close to the stage, and then stomp out in great offence at the first off-colour joke (usually within the first 90 seconds). Why he persisted in doing this for 83 performances is unknown.

they will sometimes relent and let you do it. You should try that and see if it works for you. There's a moral there,[43] you know—"The squeaky dormouse gets oiled."

[43] In the words of the Duchess, "Everything's got a moral, if only you can find it."

Chapter II.

How Alice Grew Tall.

Alice came to a long hall in the Hotel Wonderland.[44] "I wonder which floor I'm on?" she asked herself.[45]

She jumped for joy at the sight of such a very long hall to run up and down like a Wild Indian.[46] And best of all, every door was open![47] There wasn't anything in the world

44 Dodgson's favourite hotel at Freshwater Bay on the Isle of Wight, where he often stayed on his frequent summer holidays while visiting the Tennysons. It was inexplicably shelled by a U-boat in WWII, and burned to the ground. The site is now occupied by The Balti Curry Palace, an Indian restaurant.

45 Dodgson always stayed in Room 42 on the second floor. If it wasn't available he went to Blackpool.

46 Presumably a member of the First Nations (as we say in Canada), and not from the Indian subcontinent.

47 The guests in Victorian times were obviously very trusting to leave their doors

that made her happier than slamming doors. So, she slammed *every* single one of them, just as hard as she could! Which was pretty hard. Better watch your fingers, Alice!

Do you like to slam doors? Good! I didn't think you did.

Alice laughed harder and harder at all of the noise she was making. It never occurred to her that she might want a room later to take a nap and that the doors all locked as soon as she shut them.[48]

Finally, after slamming the very last door, she sat down exhausted, giggling like a mad thing. "I'll bet that woke up all the guests in the entire hotel!" she said. The thought of this made her laugh so hard that she rolled

open like this. However, the crime rate on the Isle of Wight during Victorian times was substantially less than it is today, and this makes the scene more plausible. For example, in 1873, police records indicate that there were only three crimes: the theft of a packet of fish and chips; the beating of a dead horse; and, the murder of John Duckworth (no relation to Robinson). The culprit was eventually apprehended, tried and hung. John Duckworth's murderer was never caught.

48 Dodgson has foreseen the invention of the self-locking mechanism that has made modern hotels so safe and so easy to get locked out of your room.

around on the brand-new ugly carpet, holding her tummy.

Did you ever laugh so hard that it hurt your tummy? Let me see if I can make you laugh. I'm sure that you've heard of an Elephant. I thought you had! That's right; it's the one with the long nose. And, I'm sure that you've also heard of a rhinoceros. Right again! It's the one with a long, sharp horn on the top of its nose. You're a very smart little girl! Maybe your Mother would let you come to my rooms in Oxford sometime and have tea and biscuits. Well, I'll bet you've never heard of a Hop-up-and-pot-n-Thomas,[49] have you?

There! Did that make your tummy hurt? I thought that it would. I'll bet you ca'n't say Hop-up-and-pot-n-Thomas three times real fast! Try it. Why, you can! You're a very clever little girl! Do you like bathing machines and very cold water?

---

49 First use is attributed to Heywood "Bumpus" Christian, Fort Chadbourne, Texas in 1862. How Dodgson happened to hear the term is uncertain.

"I could sure use a little nap after so much fun!" Alice said. "I'd like a room." She tried every door, but they were *all* locked. This didn't make Alice very happy. It was pitiful to see a happy face turn into a sad face. The colour of her face darkened to a horrid orange.

She noticed that someone had left their room service tray outside their door, and being very hungry, decided to investigate to see if there was anything good to eat. There was! Alice's face was suddenly happy and a bright yellow again. If she couldn't sleep she could at least eat. Do you like to eat? Me, too! In fact I'd *much* rather eat than sleep. Sleeping is so frightening, but eating is so much fun, especially if it starts with a beautiful bowl of soup. What's your favourite soup? Did you know that in The Antipathies[50] they make soup out of Kangaroo tails! Ca'n't[51] you just see the tureen hopping

[50] Dodgson's quaint way of referring to Australia.

[51] Dodgson's quaint way of abbreviating "can not", which is technically correct, but more trouble than to just spell it out. The use of "c't" hasn't yet caught on.

around on top of the table? And, in that horrid former colony of America they actually make soup out of Alligators. I'll bet they have to be *very* careful! The soup might bite them back! Aren't you glad that they don't make soup out of little girls? Of course, if they did, it would be the *best* soup in the world![52]

On the plate was a biscuit, with the words "EAT ME" written on it with grains of sugar.[53] So, Alice ate it up. If you come to my rooms in Oxford sometime I will give you a biscuit just like that one.[54]

52 Another of Dodgson's death jokes. Dodgson was fascinated by any form of oral aggression, including the ultimate one of cannibalism, something which Dr. Greenpody has made much of in his pamphlet *Oral Aggression in Erotic Children's Literature*, 1913.

53 Yet another death joke. Only a biscuit would think of telling the world that it wanted to be eaten. "DON'T EAT ME" would be a much safer message. One might reasonably ask why anyone in his or her right mind could possibly leave a perfectly good biscuit uneaten. However, this was a common practice in Victorian England, where a biscuit would be left as a tip for the Boots, who has shined the hotel guest's shoes in the middle of the night while he slept. The Victorians weren't big tippers.

54 Dodgson had a standing order for these cookies with a local Oxford baker. He went through tons of them over the years. One has survived and is in the Tannenbaum collection.

Chapter III.

The Pool of Tears.

Alice suddenly grew into the biggest happy face in the world. She grew, and grew, and she grew. Her diameter got bigger and bigger. That's what can happen when you eat a lot of biscuits,[55] especially the diameter of your waist. You have to be *very* careful, or you'll soon lose that cute little figure of yours and you'll develop horrid lumps here and

[55] Dodgson was a notoriously light eater and a frugal host. One of his early child-friends, Alison Austin, records in her reminiscences published in *The Strand* in 1902, that Dodgson once served her dinner consisting of a tiny lamb chop, a cup of weak tea, a small boiled carrot, and a biscuit. He apparently seemed quite sated, but she went home and asked for a decent sandwich.

there.[56] Being so big now, she was hungrier than ever! She checked for more biscuits up and down the length of the long hall, but there were none.

Alice was suddenly the biggest unhappy face the world had ever seen, and believe me, I've seen some very big and very unhappy faces before![57] She started to cry the world's biggest tears, each tear as big as a bucketful.[58] Soon the corridor was flooded from all of her crying, with water up past the tops of the doors.

Suddenly the White Rabbit returned, looking for something and reeking of fear?[59]

---

56 Presumably he is referring to breasts and the mature female figure in general.

57 Probably a reference to Alice Liddell's mother, who was "less than thrilled" by Dodgson's proposed marriage to Alice, or possibly a reference to the "Mrs Grundys" of the world.

58 British Imperial measure: about 9.09 litres per teardrop.

59 As Robert Ruark has noted in several of his African "Great White Hunter" novels, fear has a peculiar and disagreeable odour (not unlike steamed brussel sprouts), which is infuriating to animals, especially predators, who will often charge when they smell it. If you are afraid of dogs this is likely why they attack you. It's not that they don't like *you,* they just don't like how you *smell.* Their masters aren't afraid of them, so dogs are quite docile with them. People who are unafraid evidently smell like bacon to a dog. That's why they lick your hand or face.

He hadn't noticed Alice.

"If you please, Sir—" she said, her voice booming from the rafters, because she was so tall. This frightened the White Rabbit, who dropped his gloves and ran away, screaming that horrible high-pitched, ear-splitting noise that injured rabbits sometimes make.

Luckily, someone else's room service tray floated by. Still hungry, Alice checked it out, and found a half-full cup of tea that had "DRINK ME" printed on the side. Alice loved tea and quickly drank it down.

Alice suddenly shrank to the size of a mouse. She had to swim hard because it was *very* deep in the pool, and if she didn't she might drown—in a pool of her own tears. Can you imagine anything as sad as to drown in your own tears? Well, except that, of course![60]

Still, swimming in a pool was almost as much fun as slamming doors, and she didn't

[60] The reader must use his or her own imagination about whatever this horrid fate might be.

really care if it was her own tears! She swam and swam.

As she was swimming about she saw a brown Mouse swimming in the pool with her. This made Alice *very* happy. "Someone to play with!" she thought, never even considering if it was a sterile mouse or if it was pregnant.[61]

61 Since they were swimming in tears one would think that the entire pool would be sterile. Here again, Dodgson has foreseen the future and predicted the use of saline solutions for swimming pools, in lieu of traditional chlorination used in most modern pools. However, it is obvious from the Mouse's red eyes that it has contracted conjunctivitis, so perhaps it isn't that great of an idea.

"Oh, Mouse!" she cried. "Would you like to play?"

The Mouse was very happy to play with Alice. Would you like to play with Alice, too? I used to, and it was *ever* so much fun! And I'd like to play with you as well. Why don't we ask your Mommy if that would be all right? I know a really fun game that we could play! It's called Trigonometric Functions. If you look back at the illustration of the White Rabbit you will see that his head is a triangle. That's a plane geometric figure with three sides. With trigonometric functions you can easily calculate the lengths of the sides of his head, as well as his head's altitude. That's the distance from the bottom of his little pointed chin to the top of his furry head. That might be a very useful thing for the rabbit to know.[62]

Can you think of anything else that has "threes"? Well, there's the tripod that a camera is mounted on to keep it steady so the

[62] Exactly *how* this might be useful isn't clear.

images won't be all blurry. I was a great photographer, until that horrid Mrs Grundy[63] made me quit. For some reason she didn't like me to take pictures of little girls like you. I've given it up now for good, but I still have a marvellous collection of photographs of little girls like you. Most of them are sunbathing.[64] If you come to visit me in Oxford I will show some of them to you.

63 A fictional demonic ruler of Dante's Fifth Circle, whose task is to torment the damned on his level by shouting, for all Hell to hear, horrible gossip about their lovers and spouses. Dodgson literally imagined Mrs Grundy to be "hiding behind every bush" spying on him. This explains his strange behaviour of striking the shrubbery with his walking cane during his daily constitutionals. The rumour that he hated bushes is unfounded.

64 Of Dodgson's estimated lifetime output of 2,700 photographs, thankfully only four of nude prepubescent girls are known to have survived. The exact number of such photographs that were destroyed by the girls' parents is unknown, though it was likely in the hundreds. In the modern world one might easily expect to have to "sit next to the King's Messenger" for simply owning one, even if they are "great art," which is a matter of considerable debate and personal taste. Of course, the descendants of these little girls are understandably furious. A copy of a newly discovered Dodgson photograph of a nude child-friend might easily fetch in excess of CAD 100,000 on today's market.

CHAPTER IV.

The Caucus-Race.

"My, you *are* an excellent swimmer!" Alice remarked in a friendly tone.

The Mouse responded by screaming hideously. Do you know why? Because he had gotten a cramp in his tail! That's what happens to little girls, too, when they swim too soon after eating a biscuit.[65]

"Let's get out of the pool," the Mouse said. "My tail is very sad!"

They swam to shore, which was odd, because they were in a hotel. But things like that can

[65] Dodgson seems to imply here that he thinks that little girls have tails. Surely he was confused; everyone knows that little *boys* have those.

happen in dreams. You can be dreaming about the most wonderful thing—like Tennyson's *Maud*[66]—when all of a sudden your dream will turn on you, and out of the darkness a Jabberwock, with eyes of flame, will come whiffling[67] at you. This makes you wake up screaming your head off and feeling very *uffish*. Have you ever felt uffish? I'm sure that you have. It's how you feel when you're hungry for some tasty mutton and someone serves you Alligator Soup instead.

Well, when Alice and the Mouse crawled onto shore Alice finally got a good look at the Mouse's tail. "Your tail is certainly long, but why do you say that it's sad? It looks like a happy tail to me, except that it's perhaps a bit crooked."

"That's because there's a cramp in the fifth bend! It hurts *ever* so much!"

[66] The heroine's nickname, a shortened form of "maudlin", meaning "to be drunk enough to be emotionally silly".

[67] Most modern readers assume that this is a silly portmanteau word that Dodgson made up, but it is in fact an ancient word (1568) which means to emit or produce a light whistling puffing sound.

"Oh, do let me help adjust it!" Alice responded.

Just as the Mouse was starting to protest "Wait! I don't believe in chiro—"[68] Alice grabbed his tail and yanked it so hard that it took out *all* of the bends!

Well, the Mouse was very surprised, to say the least!

Alice and the Mouse were very wet, of course: and so were a lot of other curious creatures that had tumbled in as well. There was a Great Auk,[69] a Labrador Duck,[70] a Moa,[71] an Elephant Bird,[72] and a Do-do.[73], [74]

68 Since chiropractic wasn't invented until 1898, it is unclear what Dodgson had imagined here. Chiromancy, or palm reading, was certainly old enough, but doesn't seem to fit the context. The word 'chiropody' did not appear until 1886, still too late. The classical Greek scholar, August A. Imholtz, Jr has suggested that he was probably simply thinking of the Greek word *cheir,* meaning 'hand.' Alice *did* grab the Mouse's tail with her hands.

69 Extinct by 1844.

70 Extinct by 1870.

71 Extinct sometime in the 1600s.

72 Extinction date unknown. This was the largest bird to have ever lived, up to 9.8 feet (3 metres) high and weighing 1100 pounds (500 kg). It laid the biggest eggs ever discovered. It is quite possible that an Elephant Bird egg inspired Humpty Dumpty. The fact that he eventually fell off of the wall, broke and couldn't be put back together again is no doubt a reference to this extinction. Note that the final scene in Chapter VI of *Through the Looking-Glass* is a protracted good-bye, which seems appropriate enough when parting

73 Extinct January 14, 1898.

Do you know what an Elephant Bird is? No? Well, you *are* an ignorant child! Now, be attentive, and I'll soon cure you of your ignorance!

It's the biggest bird that ever lived.

Almost as big as an elephant! Do you think it could fly? Nor do I.

Well, do you know what was so great about the Great Auk? I don't know either. He's been extinct so long that no one can remember his notable accomplishments, if he had any, which is a very sad thing.

If you didn't know what an Elephant Bird is, then you probably won't know what a Caucus-race is either. Well, it's where you form a circle and everyone runs around it until they get dry. Even though most of the

with an animal soon to be extinct.

74 The fact that all of the creatures in the pool except Alice and the Mouse are extinct is perhaps another of Dodgson's pervasive death jokes. However, there is a touch of sadness here in that all have been swimming in a vast pool of tears. It is possible that Dodgson placed himself in the midst of extinction as a way of dealing with premonitions of his own mortality. He had, after all, caricatured himself as early as 1872 as the White Knight in *Through the Looking-Glass,* who sang a lament about an aged, aged man.

creatures were birds, not all of them could fly any better than you can, so they decided that all must run, to keep things fair.

So Alice, the Mouse and the birds set off running, and they ran round and round, till they were all quite dry again. The race took quite a long time, as none of the birds were very good runners: that's the reason they went extinct, you know. If something wants to eat you then you had better be a very good runner!

The Do-do said that *everybody* had won (something only a Do-do would say, since it rather defeats the whole purpose of a race), and *everybody* must have prizes!

Alice was the only one who had pockets, so they all decided to look in there. She had exactly five comfits and a thimble. The Do-do passed out her comfits to the Mouse and the birds, and since the thimble was all that was left presented it back to Alice, saying "We beg your acceptance of this elegant thimble!" And then all the other creatures cheered, which was a horrible noise! The air seemed full of it, and it rang through and through her head till she felt quite deafened.[75] The Elephant Bird trumpeted like an enraged pachyderm. The Great Auk squawked "Auk! Auk!" (that's the reason for its name, of course). The Moa yelled "More! More!" (and that's why they called him a Moa, you know; he never seems to get enough of anything).[76] The Labrador Duck barked. The Mouse ran and hid. Alice just stood there holding her ears, which didn't help a bit; she should have *covered* them, but in the confusion and noise she quite forgot the appropriate verb.

That thimble was a curious sort of present to give her, but when you think about it, what is a bird going to give someone? There's eggs, of course: but few birds that I have ever met give these up willingly (unlike humans, they

[75] Quoted from *Through the Looking-Glass,* Chapter VII.

[76] An insatiable appetite is one sure path to extinction, whether for an individual or an entire species.

seem to have strong avian strictures against infanticide).[77] And then, there's feathers. But most birds are even more reluctant to give those away than their eggs, as you know if you've ever tried to pluck a goose (alive *or* dead).

After Alice got her thimble back *(much* to her relief, for she valued it greatly),[78] the birds and the Mouse all wandered off, leaving Alice alone. Alice had an unhappy face once again.

[77] As the brave mother Pigeon in Chapter V of *Alice's Adventures in Wonderland,* so admirably demonstrated.

[78] There is considerable uncertainty as to exactly why. My own view is that Dodgson may have given Alice Liddell a special thimble, perhaps made of silver, and she valued it highly because of the tender memories associated with it. This seems to fit the story, where the Do-do (Dodgson) begs Alice (Alice Liddell) to accept the thimble as a present.

Chapter V.

Bill, the Lizard.

Alice was wandering up and down on the shore of the Pool of Tears when she saw the White Rabbit return, looking for his gloves. This time he saw her. She was now, as you will recall, as small as a mouse, because she had shrunk. He mistook her for his housemaid, and began ordering her about.

"Alison!" he said. You'll notice that he almost got Alice's name right, but not *quite.* "Go home this very minute, and fetch me a pair of gloves."

"He's mistaken me for his housemaid," Alice decided. So she set off to his house, which she could see in the distance.

She walked up to the door and yelled, "Knock! Knock!"

"Who's there?" asked someone on the other side.

"Alison," she lied, pretending to be the White Rabbit's housemaid.

"Alison who?" demanded the voice.

"Alison Wonderland!" she said.

Whoever (or whatever) was on the other side burst into uncontrollable laughter at the funniest joke in the whole world. She could hear him (it?) rolling around on the floor. Then she heard the back door open and close, followed by the sound of feet running. Then it was silent.[79]

---

79 There is considerable uncertainty as to the identity of this mysterious person or creature. One possibility is the mysterious Wasp from the suppressed chapter of *Through the Looking-Glass*. Another (more likely) possibility is that it was the Do-do, or Dodgson himself. As previously noted, this was his favourite joke.

"Well, since there's no one home, I'll let myself in," she said.

Up the stairs she went, straight into the White Rabbit's bedroom, which was a mess. There were psychedelic posters for a musical group called "The Looking-Glass Insects" on the wall over his bed.[80]

Just then Alice noticed a little bottle on the table, with the words "DRINK ME, DUDE!" on the label. Of course she did.

Once again, Alice grew, and she grew, and she grew. And in a very short time the room was full of Alice. There was Alice all the way up to the ceiling: and Alice in every corner of the room.[81]

---

[80] A premonition of The Beatles. See *Through the Looking-Glass,* Chapter III, and Alice's conversation with the chicken-sized Gnat: "—then you don't like all insects?" … 'I like them when they can talk,' Alice said." Here Alice is a metaphor for the multitudes of English and American girls who fell in love with the Fab Four talking and singing insects from Liverpool (which is fairly close to Blackpool, Dodgson's old holiday stomping grounds in Northwest England).

[81] A perfect metaphor for the famous "Alice Room", which once housed the enormous Lewis Carroll collection of the late Sandor Burstein, and the scene of many early meetings of the West Coast Chapter of The Lewis Carroll Society of North America.

The White Rabbit returned and when he couldn't get into his bedroom because Alice was smushed[82] up against the door, he sent Bill, the Lizard, down the chimney to investigate.

Alice, who happened to have one of her feet in the fireplace, gave a little kick and sent him flying up the chimney like a rocket.[83] I hope you don't put *your* feet in the fireplace!

Poor little Bill![84] Don't you pity him? How frightened he must have been! I once did a photograph of a little friend of mine, as a chimney sweep. She was holding a brush and *all* she had on was soot![85] I'll bet she felt like Bill.

---

82 The earliest recorded use of this portmanteau word, a combination of "smash" and "mush".

83 Dodgson doesn't make it clear if there was a fire in the hearth or not. Neither does he adequately explain how it is possible to kick a lizard up a chimney. It is extremely hard on the lizard.

84 Extinct in 1880.

85 Sadly, no copy of this photograph is known to have survived.

CHAPTER VI.

The Dear Little Puppy.

Well, Alice was still as small as a mouse, so when she came upon a Puppy it didn't look small to her *at all.* But it really *was* a *little* Puppy, you see.

When Alice met it she was understandably frightened that it might run over her. That would have been just about as bad, for *her,* as it would for *you* to be run over by a herd of Elephant Birds.

Do you have a puppy? You do? What's its name? That's a *very* cute name for a puppy! I once had a miniature schnauzer.[86] She could only understand commands in German. If I wanted her to sit, I would have to say *"Sitz!"* If I wanted her to play dead I would have to say *"Spiel tod!"* and then kick her *real* hard.[87] Can you guess what her name was? It was Alison. I used to make oatmeal porridge for her, but she wouldn't eat it unless I forced it down her throat with a big spoon.[88] Does your puppy like oatmeal-porridge? She doesn't? Even if you use a spoon?

I know a *very* funny German joke.[89] Would you like to hear it? You would? Okay. Well it

86 Dodgson obviously preferred cats (Dinah, Cheshire and Snowdrop being the most famous) to dogs.

87 Another death joke, which is particularly cruel.

88 Here Dodgson draws inspiration from "*Goldilocks and the Three Bears*." Yet another example of animal cruelty.

89 Dodgson loved German humour. *Alice's Abenteuer im Wunderland* was the second foreign language translation he arranged for, appearing in 1869, soon after the French one. He wasn't particularly fond of beer, however, and the lack of "beer" jokes in *Alice* was likely a major contributor to the poor reception of the German translation in Germany (they evidently don't find sissy "tea" jokes to be all that funny). The French love the story (or at least they say they do, in order to be as different from the Germans as possible) and they have published *almost* as many Lewis Carroll editions as the Japanese have. This is largely due to their view that Dodgson was a closet surrealist, and they have enthusiastically adopted him as one of their own. They don't find "tea" jokes all that funny either, but they seem to tolerate

goes like this: *"Klopfen! Klofpen!" "Wer ist da?" "Alison!" "Alison? Wie bitte? Was ist dein Familienname?" "Alison Wunderland!'*

Did you think that was funny? I thought you would. As they say in *Deutschland: "Das ist sehr gut!"*

---

them better.

Chapter VII.

The Blue Caterpillar.

Would you like to know what happened to Alice, after she had got away from the Puppy? It was far too large an animal, you know, for her to play with. (I don't suppose *you* would enjoy playing with a Hop-up-and-pot-n-Thomas, would you? You would always be expecting it to hop up and pot[90] or

[90] One might at first think that this was a reference to marijuana, due to the overall "druggy" context of this chapter. However, the earliest usage of "pot" as slang for marijuana appeared many years later (reportedly in Derbyshire in 1922). There is no evidence that Dodgson used any recreational drugs, except alcohol (he was responsible for the Christ Church College wine cellar). As he says, he only kept drug paraphernalia for use in creating his photography tableaus. One can see his stash in the famous photographs of Xie Kitchin in Chinese dress. Dodgson always maintained that it was tea in the chests.

something, which for an animal that large, would be a most disconcerting thing!). So Alice was very glad to run away, while it wasn't looking.

Alice decided that she was *very* tired of being so tiny, and wanted to make herself grow up to her right size again. She knew that she needed to eat or drink something: that was the regular rule,[91] you know: but she couldn't guess what thing.

However, she soon came upon a great mushroom. And seated upon it was a large Blue Caterpillar, smoking a photography prop, which is called a "hookah". Have you ever seen my famous picture of Xie Kitchen as "The Turk?"[92] You can see a hookah in that one. A hookah is ever so useful when someone in smoking <hash> tobacco. The smoke goes round and round through the long tube and cools off so that it doesn't hurt your

91 Most rules are regular by definition, so it's not certain what Dodgson is implying here: that irregular rules also exist? But if they are irregular, how can they be rules? Where is one's copy of *Symbolic Logic* when one needs it?

92 This photograph has sadly been lost.

throat. This is called "Chasing the Serpent", because the coil looks so much like a snake. Of course, I *never* chase the serpent! I'm afraid of snakes. I'll bet that you are, too, right? I thought so. You're a *very* smart little girl! You will soon find out that there are many, many things to be afraid of in life: spiders, birds, vaudeville, old age, heights, dreams, prime numbers, Mrs Liddell, Boojums, Jabberwocks, Americans, cannibals, being murdered in your bed while you're asleep, non-Euclidian geometry, boys, and other *equally* horrible things.[93]

If you look at the picture you will see the Blue Caterpillar. He doesn't look too happy. Do you know why? Because he's "blue", of course. Have you ever been blue? I have; lots of times. I live alone, which can be a very sad thing. That's why I like little girls to come and visit me—so I won't be so blue. 'Why

93 In all likelihood this is a list of Dodgson's primal fears. It's a rather long list, but in truth probably no longer than the average person's, if people were as honest as Dodgson. I would only add wasps and photo-radar to his list.

don't you ask your Mommy if it would be all right for you to come for a visit and cheer me up? I could dress you up as a Turk and you could pretend to chase snakes. That would be *very* exciting!

When Alice saw the Caterpillar she just stared and stared. She'd never seen a *blue* one before. Have you? Me neither.

"Who are you?" asked the Caterpillar.

"I hardly know," answered Alice.

"Are you happy?'

"No. I'm unhappy, because of my size."

"Then why are you smiling?"

"I'm smiling because I'm a 'happy-face'. It's my job. Why are *you* frowning?"

"I'm worried that a bird might come along and eat me," explained the Caterpillar. "Birds tend to do that with caterpillars."

"That's not too likely in your case," Alice assured him.

"Why?"

"Most things that are edible are any colour *except* blue."

The Caterpillar thought about this for a moment. "Blueberries!" it said.

"Well, except for those."

"Lobsters are blue before you cook them."

"Okay; except for blueberries and un-boiled lobsters."

"Grapes," the Caterpillar continued.

"Stop it!" Alice shouted, causing the Caterpillar to shrink up like a concertina. "Except for all of those, then. How can I grow a bit larger?"

"You have to eat. Everybody knows *that*!"

"I meant, what could I eat that would make me grow very tall, very fast?"

The Caterpillar thought again.

"Something blue," it decided.

Alice looked around. "I don't' see any blueberries, grapes or un-boiled lobsters."

"That's what I was afraid of," replied the Caterpillar.

Alice gave the Caterpillar a lean and hungry look.[94]

"You're not a bird, are you?" it asked in a *very* nervous voice.

"Of course not!"[95]

"Break off a piece of the mushroom," it said.

His was an odd instruction, but being a very obedient child she did as she was told. Do you always do as you are told? Excellent! In that case, if you come and see me we can have no end of fun.

---

94 Quoted from Dodgson's planned expurgated version of Shakespeare. This was the only fragment left after he had edited out all of the objectionable bits from *Julius Caesar*. Needless to say, by the time he had gone through all of the plays there was barely enough left for a pamphlet, and the whole project fell through.

95 Luckily for the Caterpillar they were not in The Antipathies or he might have received a different (and unpleasant) answer. "Bird" is Antipathetic slang for a "chick", which is American slang for a "broad", etc. Very few women that I have ever encountered are even the least bit inclined to eat a caterpillar, unless they happen to be pregnant or about to give birth to the Antichrist. Interestingly, they *do* eat grubs in The Antipathies. See *Alitjinya Ngura Tjukurtjarangka*, (Adelaide: University of Adelaide, 1975), where Alitji encounters a witchety grub, which the Pitjantjatjara people consider edible (the equivalent of butter in their diet). They have a saying that translates roughly as, "Better than hot witchety grubbed toast." Evidently it's an acquired taste. (A new edition of Alitji's story is forthcoming from Evertype.)

Alice looked at the piece she had broken off: it was white on the *outside,* but blue on the *inside*!"[96]

So Alice took a bite here and a nibble there, until she was exactly the same height as a Duchess, which was fortunate since that is who she is going to meet next.

[96] The Costa Rican hallucinogenic magic mushroom, *terra mirabilis* is the only known species, which fits that description.

Chapter VIII.

The Pig-Boy.

Would you like to hear about Alice's visit to see the Duchess? If not, then you can skip over to Chapter IX. But if you do, you'll miss a *very* exciting adventure, I can assure you!

Alice went up to the door and started to yell "Knock! Knock!" but someone beat her to it.

"Who's there?' she asked, familiar with how the joke goes.

"Froggy," croaked a deep voice.

"Froggy who?"

"Froggy Footman!" he croaked.

"That's not funny, at all!" Alice protested.

The door opened and a green Frog wearing a white curly wig appeared. "Why not?"

"I don't know. Comedy is hard to explain. I just know it when I hear it."

"Like what?"

"Well, jokes about death are very funny," Alice said.

"No they're not!"

"They are to *me*."

"Tell me one, and I'll see."

Alice thought for a moment. "Okay, here's one. Knock! Knock!"

Alice waited for the Frog to reply, but he just stood there staring stupidly into space.

"You're supposed to say 'Who's there?'."

"Oh! Sorry. Who's there?"

"Alice," she said.

"Alice who?"

"Alice's Adventures Underground!"

There was silence for a moment until the Frog caught it, then he started laughing and laughed for another minute. Finally he caught his breath back, and said. "I see what you mean! That is funny! Adventures underground! In a grave!"

"Yes, death can be quite humorous. At least to some people."

"Probably the living," the Frog said.

"Probably," Alice agreed.

"What do you want?" the Frog asked.

"I'd like to see the Duchess."

"You wo'n't like what you see," he warned her.

"Why?"

"She's *very* ugly. In fact, she's so ugly it will make you sneeze to see her."

"Ugly things don't make *me* sneeze," Alice said. "I've seen some *very* ugly things before and none of them made me sneeze."

"Like what?"

"Like Mrs Grundy. She's *very* ugly."

"Not as ugly as the Duchess."

"Well, I'd like to see her anyway."

"Very well. But I'd advise you to hold your nose, just in case."

Alice took hold of her nose with a firm grip and went straight into the kitchen. The Duchess sat in the middle of the room on a low stool. When Alice saw her she sneezed.

The Duchess was nursing a Piglet.

Alice took one look at it and sneezed. There was also a Cook in the back, stirring the soup.

She took one look at her and said "What's the Soup of the Day?"

"Kangaroo Tail Soup," the Cook replied. "Do you want to try a cup or a bowl?"

"No thanks. I'll just have the house salad," Alice replied. The Cook ignored her. Alice looked down near the hearth and saw a Cat—it was a Cheshire-Cat—grinning, as Cheshire-Cats always do.

"I've never seen a nicer cat!" Alice remarked. Purple was her favourite colour, you see, and she thought it looked very nice on a Cat, especially one with green eyes. Wouldn't you like to have a Cat of your own, just like that one, smiling so sweetly?

The Duchess was very rude to Alice.

"Smoking or Non-smoking?"[97] she demanded.

The Cook was not a very accomplished cook, and the room was so full of smoke that it

[97] All restaurants in Victorian England were strictly smoking. In this conversation Dodgson has thus foreseen the development of the modern restaurant setting. Dodgson wasn't a tobacco smoker, though he did own certain photography props.

made Alice's eyes sting and water. "I guess I'll take smoking," she said, as if she had any choice, then sneezed.

"It'll be a thirty-minute wait," the Duchess said.

"Why?" Alice asked, looking around. "I'm your only customer."

"Okay, then," the Duchess said.

"Now it'll be a forty-five minute wait." The Duchess glared at her, as if daring her to protest again.

"That will do fine," Alice said, realizing that if she kept arguing she would likely starve to death in a restaurant.[98] Can you imagine anything as sad as starving in a restaurant? Well, yes; there is that! I forgot about drowning in your own tears. You have an excellent memory!

Suddenly the Duchess yelled "Pig!" and threw the Shoat at Alice. She caught the Pig and ran out of the restaurant into the

98 Yet another death joke.

woods.[99] She wandered around for awhile, carrying the Piglet, which wasn't easy because it wriggled[100] about so.

The Piglet kept grunting and making rude noises, so Alice finally had to say to it, quite seriously, "Look, you little Swine, if you're going to turn into a *Boy,* I'll have nothing more to do with you!"

[99] Dodgson has foreseen the development of the forward pass in American football. This entire scene is a fairly accurate description of the game, including: players mindlessly wandering around between downs and during time-outs; the difficulties of holding onto the pigskin "because it wiggles so much" (ball handling and fumbles); the noise from the linesmen when they collide after the snap (grunting and making rude noises); spiking the ball or end zone performances after a touchdown (throwing it as far as one can); and, injuries (crawling off of the field). In addition, Dodgson emphasizes the "disgusting" nature of the whole performance and his general aversion to the ManBoy, which so typifies American professional sportsmen, forever fixated on the pursuit of adolescent games, refusing to grow up and get a dull, low-paying job like everybody else.

[100] A portmanteau word made by combining "writhed" and "wiggled". Sadly for Carrollians, this was not one that Dodgson can take credit for, since it first appeared in the 15th century. Of course, they didn't have the word "portmanteau" back then, so they didn't know what to call this case when they finally invented one; it first appeared about 1580. Up until that time everyone (except the King) used sacks. The first use of the word "portmanteau" to mean 'combining two perfectly good words to make a perfectly silly new one' was first used in 1909. Dodgson's most famous portmanteau word "Snark", is a combination of "snake" and "narcotics officer". As I pointed out in *The Hunting of the Snark,* London: Catalpa Press, 1974, the word "Bandersnatch" is a combination of "bandit", "robber", and "snatcher" (that is, a thief). Less well known is that "Alice" is a portmanteau word made up of "alert" and "mice" (that is, the antonym of "dormouse").

When she looked down into its face, what do you think she saw? It looked exactly like a Boy! Alice screamed in disgust and threw the horrid Pig-Boy as far away from her as she could.[101]

Alice watched as it crawled off. She said to herself "It made a poor shoat, but a nearly

[101] Dodgson's aversion to boys is legendary. Knowing this, his decision to make a career out of teaching mathematics to them seems to be a sure recipe for depression. The source of his deeply held disgust for boys has been the subject of much speculation and Freudian analysis. Some literary psychiatrists feel that his attitude may be an unconscious expression of self-loathing, since, after all, he was a boy himself at one time. The fact that he grew up in a family of twenty-three younger sisters may well have also had something to do with it. A superficial comparison of the bodies of prepubescent boys and girls doesn't reveal enough differences to justify his aversion for one and obsession with the other. August A. Imholtz, Jr has suggested that the fact that little boys typically only bathe once a year, and then only if thy *really* need to, may have also had something do with it. Others believe it had something to do with the fact that Dodgson just didn't care for short hair on small boys, such as the three Donkin brothers and the evil-looking Victor Alexander Lionell Parnell, Queen Victoria's godson. The few boys he seemed to tolerate were the sons of famous people he was trying to ingratiate himself with so that he could photograph them, or that had long, curly hair and looked like girls (at least from a distance, where you couldn't see the crusty dirt around their unwashed necks). Hallam Tennyson, Arthur Hughes and Sidney George Owen come to mind. As Lynne Truss has noted in her comic novel *Tennyson's Gift* (London: Hamish Hamilton, 1996), Sir Alfred didn't bother to wash his neck very often either, and is another example of the heroic Man-Boy, a concept developed to extreme length in Jackie Wullschlager's *Inventing Wonderland* (London: Methuen, 1995).

perfect Boy, I think." Do you agree with her about Boys? Me too!

CHAPTER IX.

The Cheshire-Cat.

All alone, all alone![102] Poor Alice! No Pig, and not even a horrid little Boy to keep her company.

Alice happened to look up into a tree, and there was a Cheshire-Cat perched on a high branch (where it could jump off onto the back of any little girl that might happen by

[102] It has been suggested that this is an unconscious lament by Dodgson concerning his bachelorhood. He wasn't completely alone, of course, even after the deaths of his parents; there were always his twenty-three sisters cloistered away in Guilford. He often visited them, but this was strictly familial, and he was still lonely in this virtual crowd of siblings. He is reported to have said that "going to Guilford for the weekend is like visiting a nunnery, except not nearly as much fun." His sisters idolized Tennyson and would sit around in the evening quoting lines from one poem or the other.

unsuspecting, like a doe or a fawn). Little girls should always keep their eyes open for any Cheshire-Cats in trees.

The Cat had a *very* nice smile, no doubt: but just look what a lot of very sharp teeth it's got! It looks frightfully dangerous. I wonder if it likes to eat little girls? Some cats do, you know: especially Tigers in India and Lions in Derbyshire (they often escape from traveling Circuses, you know). How would *you* like to be badly bitten by a vicious girl-eating Cat? Ouch! Do you know what Cats think about little girls? They think that they're "purrrfectly" delicious! So do I.[103]

Well, it couldn't help having teeth, you know: and it *could* have helped smiling, supposing it had been Cross. So, on the whole, she was glad to see it.

At this moment the Cheshire-Cat spoke to Alice. "Do you see that flower growing there at the base of this tree?"

This was an odd question to come from a Cat, so Alice looked very closely.

"Yes," she said. "It's a Fox-Glove," showing the Cat how clever she was to know the names of such things.

"No indeed!" said the Cat. "*Foxes* never wear gloves."[104]

"What is it then?"

"It's a Folk's-Glove," the Cat said.

---

[103] Oral aggression expressed as an attack by a trusted pet, perhaps the worst sort of betrayal. And cannibalism again. For a detailed analysis of Cheshire-Cat dentition see Alitji Sewell's fascinating article, "Skulls of the Cheshire-Cats," in *Scientific Alician,* 1980. The fact that Tenniel's Cheshire-Cat has so many teeth makes his image particularly frightening to "Children aged Nought to Five".

[104] But rabbits do? See Chapter III. *There's* logic for you!

"What's *that* supposed to mean?"

"That refers to Fairies. They're called 'the good *Folk*'."

"I don't believe in fairies."[105]

"Why not?"

"I ca'n't see them," Alice explained.

At this the Cheshire-Cat slowly vanished away; except for his *voice.* "Can you see me?" it asked.

"Well, no; not at the moment."

"So, I suppose you no longer believe in me then."

"I still believe in you. I *did* see you earlier."

[105] Alice might not have, but there is no doubt that Dodgson believed in their literal existence. He wasted his last creative energies on the dreadful *Sylvie and Bruno* books. He doesn't make a very convincing argument. Dodgson regarded the *Alice* books as "fairy tales", as evidenced by the prefatory poem for *Through the Looking-Glass,* where he refers to "the love-gift of a fairy tale". If you go into any modern bookstore searching for Lewis Carroll books you won't find them in the "Fairy Tales" section, which is reserved for stories by authors such as Grimm and Andersen. The *Alice* books are usually pigeonholed with the "Classics". And lots of luck if you're trying to find a copy of *Sylvie and Bruno.* That's been relegated to literary obscurity, along with *The Nursery "Alice".* One wonders how Dodgson, an ordained Anglican minister, managed to reconcile his Christian beliefs with his belief in the existence of fairies. If he expects to find them in Heaven, then he's likely going to be very disappointed. They *might* be in the "basement" compartment of eternity, however.

"So, let me get this straight; you only believe in things you can see or have seen. Is that your position?"

"Yes."

"Well, what about the wind? Do you believe in that?"

"Of course not," Alice said, to the Cat's surprise.

"Let me guess: you must believe that the air stays perfectly still while the world rushes through it."

"Exactly."

"How about gravity? Do you believe in that?"

"Of course not," Alice said. "One ca'n't believe impossible things."[106]

"I see. Then I assume that you must believe that the world is always rushing straight up, and that's what keeps you from falling off of it."

"Exactly."

[106] As Alice says to the White Queen in Chapter V of *Through the Looking-Glass.*

"In that case, I'd advise against your ever visiting The Antipathies," said the Cat.[107]

"Believe me; I never plan to journey there."

"Why?"

"I read that they eat grubs there."

"Are you a Grub?" it asked.

"Of course not!"

"Then why are you worried about that?"

"Are you a Fairy?" Alice asked, deciding to change the subject. She didn't like talking about worms.

"Of course!"

"I thought you might be," Alice said. "Though I must admit that I had always imagined that fairies looked like little naked children with dragonfly or butterfly wings attached at their shoulders."

"That's *exactly* how most of them look. I'm an exception. I thought you said that you didn't believe in Fairies because you hadn't

[107] Another death joke, this one resulting in falling off of the earth into deep space. Have you been counting?

ever seen them. If you haven't seen them, then how do you know what they look like?"

"I've seen their pictures in some books, but I don't remember where."

"I see."

"I've always wondered. Are Fairies good?"

"They're quite good, actually; they taste lovely!"

Alice let out a little shriek of horror. "Do you actually eat them?" She was incredulous.

The Cheshire-Cat's grinning mouth suddenly reappeared (you will recall that he was still invisible, and that the only thing that could be seen was his *voice* hanging in the air like alphabetical laundry put out to dry). "I have teeth don't I?"

"You have a *great many* teeth, but I had no idea they were for chewing fairies."

"Fairies make an excellent snack. They're crunchy, have very few calories and have a salty taste.[108] Have you ever seen a cat catch and eat a Grasshopper?"

"Yes, many times: in our garden."

"No you haven't. Cats hate the taste of Grasshoppers and they *never* eat them. You've actually watched them catching and eating Fairies; you just *thought* they were grasshoppers." The rest of the Cat reappeared.

Suddenly something occurred to Alice. "Am I a Fairy?"

"You certainly *look* like one," the Cat said.

"I was afraid of that!"

"But I suspect that you're really only a dream. So I'm thinking that perhaps you

108 Dodgson had foreseen the essential elements for the perfect snack food, including popcorn (as long as you leave off the butter).

aren't really edible, after all. You can eat in your dreams, but you ca'n't eat a dream. Are you a dream-girl?"

"Well, I'm certainly in a dream, so I suppose that makes me one."

"Probably. Too bad, really. You look purr-fectly delicious!"

Alice decided it was time to go, before the Cat decided to change his mind. "Would you please tell me which way I ought to go from here?"

"The Hatter lives over that way," it said, pointing with one of its paws, "and the March Hare over that way. They're both mad! Visit whichever you like." Having said this it vanished, much to Alice's relief.

Chapter X.

The Mad Tea-Party.

Alice set off at once to visit the March Hare and the Hatter.[109] She found them having tea under a great tree, with a Do-Re-Mi-Mouse sitting between them. Do you know what a Do-Re-Mi-Mouse is?

That's a Mouse that sings in its sleep. You've probably heard someone talk in his or her sleep before, haven't you? I thought so. Sometimes they say the funniest things! I've

109 Dodgson doesn't emphasize the Hatter's madness in either *Alice in Nurseryland* or *The Nursery "Alice"* evidently considering the concept of an insane hat salesman much too frightening for a "Child aged Nought to Five" to contemplate. This is an odd sort of censorship in a book filled with death jokes, cannibalism, nightmares, pet abuse, and fairycide.

done it myself, lots of times. But you've probably never heard anyone *sing* in his or her sleep, right? Do you know what they sing? That's right! They always sing lullabies. You're a very clever little girl. That's why they're so sleepy, you know. Every time they try to wake up they hear themselves singing a lullaby and go right back to sleep. It's like a trap.[110] I'm glad I'm not a Do-Re-Mi-Mouse! I hate sleeping. It would be better to be a March Hare or a Hatter, and never have to sleep.[111]

There were only these three at the table, but there were quantities of teacups set all along it. You can see the March Hare, with his long ears wrapped up in straw, the Hatter with his

[110] Dodgson has accurately described the sensations and difficulties of coming out of a coma. This was the accepted medical explanation given in medieval medical textbooks up until about 1650.

[111] Dodgson doesn't seem to realize that they are mad *because* they suffer from sleep depravation, due to the fact that it's always teatime, and never bedtime. Never sleeping has its advantages, however. Isaac Asimov, one of the most prolific authors who ever lived, and who would typically write five books simultaneously, only got an estimated sixteen hours of sleep between the age of 18 and his death.

silly hat with the price tag still on, and the Do-Re-Mi-Mouse in the illustrations.

Alice went over and sat down at the table as there were *plenty* of empty seats. "No room!" they all shouted, which was a lie. Don't you just hate liars? That's what I hate the most about that dreadful Mrs Grundy; she's always telling lies about me.[112] I *never* took any photographs of little girls sunbathing without

112 Dodgson proceeds to present an impassioned self-defence. The "kissing" incident often referred to was a genuine mistake. The seventeen-year old girl was in fact a young actress dressed in costume on her way to the theatre, where she was to appear as the eleven-year old heroine in *Tusker!* Still, it was a serious breach of etiquette and a regrettable incident that Dodgson never successfully managed to resolve, even with a complimentary copy of *Alice's Adventures in Wonderland*, which he had specially bound in an embarrassing purple cloth with designs embossed in guilt. This spectacular copy is now in the private collection of Edward Wakeling, along with half of the Lewis Carroll books in England. The copy is inscribed: "From the Author, with sincere regrets for any embarrassment I might have inadvertently caused. 'I weep for you,' the Walrus said, 'I deeply sympathize.' With sobs and tears I ask your forgiveness. The Do-Do." A careful analysis of the .various Lewis Carroll biographies reveals that he in fact made four *very* serious mistakes: a) not waiting until Alice Liddel was a bit older before asking for her hand in marriage; b) not changing his bedding frequently enough to avoid migraines; c) keeping a diary (it has made it much too easy for forgers to create genuine-looking inscriptions; one estimates that well over half of the inscribed editions attributed to Lewis Carroll are in fact forgeries); and, d) writing those horrid *Sylvie and Bruno* books. The last was by far the most egregious. Who can stand to listen to Bruno talk, even in your mind when you read it silently? There *is* some excellent poetry in them, however. One just wishes that he had simply published a book of poems.

their parents' permission, no matter what she says. And I have only once ever kissed a girl over seventeen, and that was dreadful mistake that I shall never, never make again, I can assure you![113] It was an *honest* mistake. Do you ever make *really* serious mistakes? I thought so. Most people *do,* at least once or twice in their lives. I believe that the rule is that you are allowed at least three really serious mistakes before they draw-and-quarter you. And you should realize that it is dreadfully easy to make them, if you're not *very* careful! It's like making three not-so-clever wishes when you've released a jinni from a bottle. You'd like to go back and try it again, but the regular rule is "What's done is done." And if you've done it, you just have to live with it for the rest of your miserable life![114] The Mrs Grundys of the world are a

[113] This would seem to explain why he never proposed marriage to Gurdy Thomson, the close friend and companion of the last years of his life. She likely would have married him in an instant, had he asked her, which, of course, he didn't. She was probably simply a tad too lumpy.

[114] As the Red Queen said to Alice in *Through the Looking-Glass,* Chapter IX,

hard-hearted, mean-spirited bunch of old busybodies who don't have an ounce of forgiveness among the nasty lot of them! Excuse my French!

CHAPTER XI.

The Queen's Garden.

The Queen of Hearts[115] had a lovely little garden. I say it was little because the Queen herself was quite small: only about as high as a mouse standing up on its hind legs. Alice was even smaller, having shrunk down earlier. In the garden was a *very* small rose tree. In addition there were tiny gardeners who looked rather like men, except they were really live playing cards, with heads and arms and legs on them so that they *looked* like men.

[115] In Dodgson's case, the *real* Queen of Hearts was Alice Pleasance Liddell. Other child-friends were just princesses.

When Alice left the Mad Tea-Party she wandered into this little garden and came upon the little gardeners at work painting the five white blossoms on the rose tree with red paint.[116] This was because these poor little gardeners had planted a *white* one by mistake; and they were frightened about it, because the Queen was *sure* to be angry and would then order their heads to be cut off!

She was a dreadfully savage Queen, and that was the way she always did, when she was angry with people.[117] "Off with their heads!" she would command. They didn't *really* cut their heads off, you know: because

[116] Curiously, in *The Nursery "Alice"*, Dodgson also says "there were *five* large white roses on the tree—" However, there are six open blossoms that are clearly visible in Tenniel's illustration. Even though Dodgson was an accomplished mathematician, he evidently couldn't count to six. He likely discovered this error, but couldn't bear the financial loss of reprinting the sheets yet again, and just lived with the embarrassment.

[117] This is quite likely a metaphor for Alice Liddle's mother. Dodgson often played croquet with the Dean and Mrs Liddle in their garden before he got in deep trouble with Mrs Liddle. One popular theory is that he made the mistake of croqueting her ball into the rose bushes just one time too many. It may have been fun at the moment, but one has to wonder if it was *really* worth it.

nobody ever obeyed her: but that was what she always said.[118]

Right in the middle of painting the white roses the Queen showed up with all of her retinue. She went over to examine what the gardeners were doing. When she touched one of the roses she got red paint on the royal fingers and this made her *very* angry![119]

"Off with their heads!" she bellowed, like a Bull Moose in the rutting season. Do you know what the *rutting season* is? No? Well, I'll explain it to you. It happens in the Fall, when some of the younger Bull Moose get very agitated about not being married yet. They spend all of their time standing in the middle of the forest bellowing at the Girl Moose (that's more than one Moose, in this case; it's

[118] If you've ever dug through your things for a pack of cards, only to find that one or two cards are missing from the deck and wondered why, this likely explains it. They *do* cut their heads off, in spite of Dodgson's assurances to the contrary. Why Dodgson tried to cover up their savage judicial system is unclear.

[119] The Queen clearly states that this is what she is angry about, not because the rose-tree had white blossoms. If the paint had just dried a little quicker, 'all would have been well.

a very peculiar plural') who might happen to be within hearing distance, yelling, "Does anyone want to dance?" The Bull will keep doing this and doing this, night and day, but of course no one in their right mind, not even a Girl Moose, wants to dance with a Bull Moose. But the Bull keeps on yelling it anyway. Anyone within hearing distance finally says, "I wish that Moose would shut up! He's in a terrible rut!" There: now you know! Just be glad God didn't make you a Moose instead of a little girl!

If you look at the illustration you will see what the Queen of Hearts looks like. My! She is so angry that her face is *very* red. Do you think her head might explode? I wouldn't be surprised. If it does, then everyone else will have the satisfaction of yelling "Off with her head!" as it takes off like a sky-rocket.[120]

---

[120] This is a particularly gruesome death joke, which echoes the plight of Bill, the Lizard.

Chapter XII.

The Lobster-Quadrille.

Did you ever play Croquet?[121] There are large wooden balls, painted with different colours, that you have to roll about; and arches of wire that you have to send them through; and great wooden mallets, with long handles, to knock the balls about with.

121 Dodgson was an accomplished croquet player and swung a mean mallet. He was Captain of the Christ Church Croquet Team, "The Flamingos." He lobbied hard to get his team to wear boaters and pink sweaters, but his teammates would have none of it. Dodgson invented a number of variations on the game, to be played on different types of terrain: shingle, meadows, barnyards, mountains, and college libraries. By far the most exciting was Library Croquet, because of the riots that often ensued; the players usually defeated the outraged readers, since they were much better armed, having brought mallets with them.

Well, that's the *regular* game, but in Wonderland they play a slight variation. Instead of mallets they use Flamingos,[122] and for balls they use *live* Hedgehogs,[123] which roll up into balls.

Alice had a great deal of trouble with her cantankerous Flamingo, which had the infuriating habit of suddenly going limp on her. And her hedgehog would, for no apparent reason, just get up and wander off.

If you talk your Mommy into letting you come and visit me in Oxford (whining often helps convince them) I shall be very happy to teach you how to play this wonderful game.

122 Named after the obsolete Spanish word *flamengo,* which is now *flamenco,* meaning "to stand on one leg until one falls over." Dodgson often used this avian technique in trying to stay awake for extended periods of time. This is likely the reason he selected this bird for the mallet, instead of, for example, the crow, which has a great deal of trouble in standing on one foot.

123 It's odd that Dodgson felt compelled to point out that they were using *live* ones, as opposed to *dead* ones. By distinguishing this for the hedgehogs one has to assume that they must have been using *dead* flamingos. They probably were. Very few flamingos migrate through England. Most of the flamingos in use by the Victorians (for God only knows what purpose) were imported from Kenya in a stuffed condition. Hedgehogs are presently an endangered species in England, the result of over a hundred years of croquet and being run over on highways by lorries (aptly named after the loris, an infuriatingly slow moving nocturnal creature).

After Alice had played for awhile she met the Duchess on the playing field, and stopped to talk with her for a few minutes. This time she wasn't quite as rude as before, probably because she was off work and more relaxed.

They talked about morals and other deep philosophical issues. Alice's face started to turn from a happy yellow colour to a shade of orange. You know what that means! Right! She was starting to get unhappy again.

Luckily, the Queen came up and chased the Duchess away. "Have you met the Gryphon and the Mock Turtle yet?" she asked in a surprisingly pleasant tone. Alice was a bit surprised that her head hadn't blown off, and that her facial colour had lightened to a soft pink.

"She must be winning," Alice thought. "No, I haven't," she said aloud. "In fact I don't even know what they are."

You don't know what a Gryphon[124] is?

[124] In describing Tenniel's famous illustration in *The Nursery "Alice"*, Dodgson curiously says that the Gryphon has "green scales", yet Tenniel has clearly

Well! Do you know *anything?* That's the question. It's a fabulous looking monster with the head and wings of an Eagle stuck onto the body of a Lion. Its head and feet are red and the rest of it is green. I have no idea where they came up with such a silly name for it. If they had asked *me* what to call it I would have told them to call it a Christmas Decoration. It makes a crazy looking animal, but would look just fine on a Christmas tree.

A Mock Turtle is another fabulous monster, with the head, hind legs and tail of a calf, all stuffed into the shell and front flippers of a Sea Turtle. Don't ask *me* how they manage to do *that!* Do you know the reason they call it a *Mock Turtle?* Are you ready for this? Well, you've probably eaten Turtle soup, haven't you? I thought you had. They make it out of turtles of course. Well, Mock Turtle soup is made out of the head of a calf! Can you

drawn it with typical feathers, as appropriate for the upper body of an eagle. Perhaps Dodgson had a premonition of the modern discussion about the evolution of birds from dinosaurs.

imagine what a horrible thing *that* is to do to a *baby,* even if it is just a Cow?

Alice went over to meet them. The Queen commanded the Mock Turtle and the Gryphon to dance the Lobster-Quadrille[125] for Alice. Since they had little choice, they

125 For some reason, Dodgson didn't feel it necessary to explain what a Lobster-Quadrille is (even though he did with croquet), so it must have been common knowledge, even to "Children aged Nought to Five".

hopped to it, managing to tread on Alice's toes in the process.[126]

[126] It isn't known if Dodgson was an accomplished dancer or not. However, it seems unlikely. The only females that he would have been inclined to dance with would have been little girls, which, for a tall man like Dodgson, would have been a bit awkward at best. Like many things (marriage, fatherhood, military service, sex, rugby, prizefighting, polo, arctic exploration, deep-sea diving, etc.) he remained the perennial observer, not the active participant. The fact that the Gryphon and the Mock Turtle tread on Alice's toes quite possibly refers in a light-hearted way to an actual incident in which Dodgson attempted to dance with Alice Liddell with the same disastrous result.

CHAPTER XIII.

Who Stole the Tarts?

I imagine that you must have heard that the Queen of Hearts made some tarts. And you have probably also heard that the Knave of Hearts stole them all away. I thought you had!

Because of this they took him prisoner, put chains on his wrists so that he couldn't get away, and took him before the King of Hearts, so that there could be a regular trial. I feel sorry for the Knave. Life is full of trials, and I've had plenty, so I deeply sympathize! For example, there's the difficulty of making collodian[127] plates for taking photographs, as well as getting the sitters to hold perfectly still for a few minutes. You were often tempted to put your subject's head in a vice! And there's the terrible (and expensive) difficulty of getting the printers to print sheets for books that aren't all smudgy. I've had trials with: unreasonable mothers who didn't want to lend me their young daughters for the Summer; keeping my teeth perfectly clean;[128] keeping my real name secret (I have a secret to tell you: it's really Wilfred P. Smudgeon![129] Don't tell *anyone*!); little girls

[127] A thick solution of pyroxylin, a flammable mixture of nitrocellulose. It's lucky Dodgson didn't burn down the College coating his plates! Some people believe that Dodgson didn't take that many photographs of little boys because he detested them. Of course he did, but the truth of the matter is that they were genetically incapable of holding still long enough for the exposure. Dodgson likely just gave up on the bad idea.

[128] Dodgson visited his dentist every day, something that has convinced many people that he was a masochist. One can only assume that he must have good insurance! He would certainly have loved the waterpic and fluoridation. No one knows exactly how many cavities he had, but likely very few indeed.

[129] It is unclear why Dodgson would have identified himself as actually being this person. There are only three British citizens with this odd name known to have resided in England from 1830-1880: a) William Perry Smudgeon (1846–1873), a Derbyshire tinker, dentist and book collector; b) William Philpot Smudgeon, a London petty thief (?–1876), who was hung after being convicted of the theft of a cucumber frame; and, c) William Percy Smudgeon

growing up and getting all lumpy; Non-Euclidean geometry;[130] and too many more to even bother you with. Let's just say that I've had *plenty* of trials, and leave it at that.

If you look at the illustration you can see the King of Hearts. Doesn't he look *grand?* But he doesn't look happy. You can tell because

(1871-1906), a child actor best known for his performance as the Dormouse in Savile Clarke's production of *Alice in Wonderland* (he tragically fell to his death from a wire, while performing a flying stunt as Puck).

130 Which he didn't believe in, though you will recall that he *did* believe in fairies.

his face isn't yellow. It's probably because the crown is so heavy.

The Queen isn't happy either. In fact, her blood pressure is up and her face is all red again. Everybody had best be on their best behaviour!

The White Rabbit has changed clothes and is all dressed up. He has a little trumpet to blow when he needs to get the creatures' attention, which he does right now. This is what he read:

"The Queen of Hearts, she made some tarts:[131]
All on a summer day:
The Knave of Hearts, he stole those tarts,
And took them quite away!"[132]

[131] Dr Selwyn Goodacre has noted that Dodgson used a colon in *The Nursery "Alice"*, but a comma in *Alice's Adventures in Wonderland.* The exact significance of this *IS* a matter of great uncertainty.

[132] Thus, the charges are specifically petty theft and transportation of stolen property. Nowhere is the Knave of Hearts accused of actually *eating* them, which is a good thing, since he would have then also been charged with the much more serious offence of disposing of stolen property.

The Jury is in the Jury-box. They will have to decide if the Knave is "guilty" or "not guilty".

The White Rabbit blew his little trumpet and called out "Alice!"

Alice jumped up and when she did she tipped over the Jury-box and spilled out all of the Jurors. It took her quite awhile to get them all back in their places, especially the

Elephant Bird, who was one of them. You will recall that he was a *very* big bird.

The rest of the Jurors were: the Great Auk, the Labrador Duck, the Do-Do, a Mouseling, the Moa, the Do-Re-Mi-Mouse, the Pig-Boy, a Pigeon, a Flamingo, a Hedgehog, and a Storkling.

Do you know what a *Storkling* is? Why, it's a little baby stork. So, what do you think that a *Mouseling* is then? You're right! A baby Mouse! You're a *very* clever little girl! So, now that you know what a Storkling and a Mouseling are, what do you think a *Crawling* is?

No, silly! A Crawling isn't a little "*Craw*". Crawling is how you move about on all fours before you learn to walk.

Chapter XIV.

The Shower of Cards.

Oh dear, oh dear![133] What is it all about? And what's happening to Alice?

[133] This is the White Rabbit's famous quotation from Chapter I. This, and "I'm late! I'm late!", are the third most often quoted expressions ever spoken by a rabbit in the English language (no one knows what the most common one is in Rabbit-talk except the rabbits). The first and second most often quoted rabbit expressions are, of course, "Ehhh, what's up, Doc?" and "Of course you know, *this* means war!" by Bugs Bunny. Nothing else even comes close to those two. Many readers mistakenly attribute the expression "Oh, dear!" to Piglet, Winnie the Pooh's timid friend, but he stole it from the White Rabbit. Walt Disney's famous parody, "I'm late! I'm late! For a very important date!" is yet another American piracy, though a catchy one. See Alison Tannenbaum's monumental work, *Rabbits Say the Darndest Things!* (Dead Deer: Storkling Press, 1984). It may be of interest to note these other Carrollian rabbit quotations, spoken by the March Hare, that have also made the list: No. 31, "No room! No room!" (possibly inspired by the Christmas story); No. 63, "Have some more wine." (a common phrase in European opera); No. 207, "You might as well say … that 'I like what I get,' is the same thing as 'I get what I like'!" (a favourite expression of Bill Gates, who has the money to make it happen); No. 605: "I told you butter wouldn't suit the

Well, I'll tell you all about it, as well as I can.[134] The way the trial ended was this. The King wanted to settle whether the Knave had taken the tarts or somebody else had taken them. But the wicked[135] *Queen* wants to have his *punishment* settled, first of all. That wasn't at all fair, *was* it? Because, you know,

works!" (sometimes used by airplane mechanics in interviews conducted by the FAA following a plane crash); No. 712: "It was the *best* butter" (adopted by the American Dairy Association as their motto in 1953; it was replaced in 1962 by "Cholesterol and Bovine Hormones are *Good* for You!"); and, No. 8,307: "Were you happy in prison, dear child?" This is spoken by Haigha in Chapter VII of *Through the Looking-Glass,* the only quote making the list from this character, better known for his miming abilities. The quotation is sometimes heard outside penal institutions, especially in the United States, which maintains one of the world's largest prison systems. Approximately half of those incarcerated in U.S. Federal penitentiaries are there for possession of photography props.

134 A blatant lie. Dodgson has left out almost everything that happened in the original story. It has been well established that lying to children can be extremely damaging to their psyches and can result in the inability to tell the truth in their adult lives. My parents lied to me *once* (I was told that the stork delivered me; I now know that it was really the Easter Bunny). So, you can blame them for most of this present work (an aromatic blend of fact and fiction, with a distinct nutty aftertaste) if you have to find someone to blame.

135 Here and in *The Nursery "Alice"* are the only place that Dodgson characterizes the Queen of Hearts as being 'wicked.' This is another indication that Dodgson considered *Alice's Adventures in Wonderland* to be a fairy tale. The ultimate villain in many fairy tales is a 'wicked Queen' (not merely an angry one). Dodgson later applies this same pejorative to the ultimate villain in his own life, Mrs Grundy.

supposing he never *took* the Tarts, then he oughtn't to be executed.

Have *you* ever been punished for something you haven't done? Really? So have I; many times: but then I've already told you about the wicked Mrs Grundy.

Since it wasn't fair, Alice said "Stuff and nonsense!" The Queen's face went square with rage and she yelled "Off with her head!" (Just what she always said, when she was angry.)

So Alice said "Who cares for you? You're nothing but a pack of cards!"

This made them all angry and they flew up into the air, and came tumbling down again, all over Alice, just like a shower of rain.

This caused Alice to wake up. She found out that the cards were only leaves off the tree that the wind had blown down upon her face.

Wouldn't it be a nice thing to have a curious dream, just like Alice?

Why don't you ask your Mommy one *last* time to *please, please* let you visit me at Oxford, or Eastbourne, or London, so you can tell me *all* about your own curious dreams?

Good-bye, Alice dear, good-bye!

SOURCES

Alice's Adventures in Wonderland, by Lewis Carroll, 2015

Alice's Adventures in Wonderland, illus. June Lornie, 2013

Alice's Adventures in Wonderland, illus. Mathew Staunton, 2015

Alice's Adventures in Wonderland, illus. Harry Furniss, 2016

Through the Looking-Glass and What Alice Found There,
by Lewis Carroll 2009

The Nursery "Alice", by Lewis Carroll, 2015

Alice's Adventures under Ground, by Lewis Carroll, 2009

The Hunting of the Snark, by Lewis Carroll, 2010

SEQUELS

A New Alice in the Old Wonderland, by Anna Matlack Richards, 2009

New Adventures of Alice, by John Rae, 2010

Alice Through the Needle's Eye, by Gilbert Adair, 2012

Wonderland Revisited and the Games Alice Played There,
by Keith Sheppard, 2009

SPELLING

Alice's Adventures in Wonderland,
Retold in words of one Syllable by Mrs J. C. Gorham, 2010

𐐈𐑊𐐮𐑅'𐑆 𐐈𐐼𐑂𐐯𐑌𐐽𐐲𐑉𐑆 𐐮𐑌 𐐎𐐲𐑌𐐼𐐲𐑉𐑊𐐰𐑌𐐼,
Alice printed in the Deseret Alphabet, 2014

𐐜 𐐐𐐲𐑌𐐻𐐮𐑍 𐐲𐑂 𐑄 𐑅𐑌𐐪𐑉𐐿,
The Hunting of the Snark printed in the Deseret Alphabet, 2016

Alice's Adventures in Wonderland,
Alice printed in Dyslexic-Friendly fonts, 2015

ALICE'S ADVENTURES IN A DYSLEXIC WONDERLAND,
Alice printed in a font that simulates Dyslexia, 2015

Alice printed in the Ewellic Alphabet, 2013

'Ælɪsɪz Əd'ventʃəz ɪn 'Wʌndəˌlænd,
Alice printed in the International Phonetic Alphabet, 2014

Alis'z Advnčrz in Wunḍland, *Alice* printed in the Ñspel orthography, 2015

Alice printed in the Nyctographic Square Alphabet, 2011

Alice printed in the Shaw Alphabet, 2013

ALISIZ ADVENCƎRZ IN WUNDRLAND,
Alice printed in the Unifon Alphabet, 2014

Scholarship

Elucidating Alice: A Textual Commentary on *Alice's Adventures in Wonderland*, by Selwyn Goodacre, 2015

Behind the Looking-Glass: Reflections on the Myth of Lewis Carroll, by Sherry L. Ackerman, 2012

Selections from the Lewis Carroll Collection of Victoria J. Sewell, compiled by Byron W. Sewell, 2014

Satires

Clara in Blunderland, by Caroline Lewis, 2010

Lost in Blunderland: The further adventures of Clara, by Caroline Lewis, 2010

John Bull's Adventures in the Fiscal Wonderland, by Charles Geake, 2010

The Westminster Alice, by H. H. Munro (Saki), 2010

Alice in Blunderland: An Iridescent Dream, by John Kendrick Bangs, 2010

Simulations

Davy and the Goblin, by Charles Edward Carryl, 2010

The Admiral's Caravan, by Charles Edward Carryl, 2010

Gladys in Grammarland, by Audrey Mayhew Allen, 2010

Alice's Adventures in Pictureland, by Florence Adèle Evans, 2011

Folly in Fairyland, by Carolyn Wells, 2016

Rollo in Emblemland, by J. K. Bangs & C. R. Macauley, 2010

Phyllis in Piskie-land, by J. Henry Harris, 2012

Alice in Beeland, by Lillian Elizabeth Roy, 2012

Eileen's Adventures in Wordland, by Zillah K. Macdonald, 2010

Sewelliana

Sun-hee's Adventures Under the Land of Morning Calm,
by Byron & Victoria Sewell, 2016

선희의 조용한 아침의 나라 모험기
(Seonhuiui joyonghan achim-ui nala moheomgi),
Sun-hee in Korean, tr. Miyeong Kang, 2016

Alix's Adventures in Wonderland:
Lewis Carroll's Nightmare, by Byron W. Sewell, 2011

Áloþk's Adventures in Goatland, by Byron W. Sewell, 2011

Alice's Bad Hair Day in Wonderland, by Byron W. Sewell, 2012

The Carrollian Tales of Inspector Spectre, by Byron W. Sewell, 2011

Alice in Nurseryland, by Byron W. Sewell, 2016

The Haunting of the Snarkasbord, by Alison Tannenbaum,
Byron W. Sewell, Charlie Lovett, & August A. Imholtz, Jr, 2012

Snarkmaster, by Byron W. Sewell, 2012

In the Boojum Forest, by Byron W. Sewell, 2014

Murder by Boojum, by Byron W. Sewell, 2014

Close Encounters of the Snarkian Kind, by Byron W. Sewell, 2016

TRANSLATIONS

Alice's Adventures in An Appalachian Wonderland,
Alice in Appalachian English, tr. Byron & Victoria Sewell, 2012

Patimatli ali Alice tu Văsilia ti Ciudii,
Alice in Aromanian, tr. Mariana Bara, 2015

Алесіны прыгоды ў Цудазем'і (Alesiny pryhody u Tsudazem'i), *Alice* in Belarusian, tr. Max Ščur, 2016

На тым баку Люстра і што там напаткала Алесю (Na tym baku Liustra i shto tam napatkala Alesiu), *Looking-Glass* in Belarusian, tr. Max Ščur, 2016

Снаркаловы (Snarkalovy),
The Hunting of the Snark in Belarusian, tr. Max Ščur, 2016

Crystal's Adventures in A Cockney Wonderland,
Alice in Cockney Rhyming Slang, tr. Charlie Lovett, 2015

Aventurs Alys in Pow an Anethow,
Alice in Cornish, tr. Nicholas Williams, 2015

Alice's Ventures in Wunderland,
Alice in Cornu-English, tr. Alan M. Kent, 2015

Alices Hændelser i Vidunderlandet, *Alice* in Danish, tr. D.G., Forthcoming

آلیس در سرزمین عجایب (Âlis dar Sarzamin-e Ajâyeb),
Alice in Dari, tr. Rahman Arman, 2015

La Aventuroj de Alicio en Mirlando,
Alice in Esperanto, tr. E. L. Kearney, 2009

La Aventuroj de Alico en Mirlando,
Alice in Esperanto, tr. Donald Broadribb, 2012

Trans la Spegulo kaj kion Alico trovis tie,
Looking-Glass in Esperanto, tr. Donald Broadribb, 2012

Les Aventures d'Alice au pays des merveilles,
Alice in French, tr. Henri Bué, 2015

Les Aventures d'Alice au pays des merveilles,
Alice in French, tr. Henri Bué, illus. Mathew Staunton, 2015

ელისის თავგადასავალი საოცრებათა ქვეყანაში
(Elisis t'avgadasavali saoc'rebat'a k'veqanaši),
Alice in Georgian, tr. Giorgi Gokieli, 2016

Alice's Abenteuer im Wunderland,
Alice in German, tr. Antonie Zimmermann, 2010

Die Lissel ehr Erlebnisse im Wunnerland,
Alice in Palantine German, tr. Franz Schlosser, 2013

Der Alice ihre Obmteier im Wunderlaund,
Alice in Viennese German, tr. Hans Werner Sokop, 2012

Balþos Gadedeis Aþalhaidais in Sildaleikalanda,
Alice in Gothic, tr. David Alexander Carlton, 2015

Nā Hana Kupanaha a 'Āleka ma ka 'Āina Kamaha'o,
Alice in Hawaiian, tr. R. Keao NeSmith, 2012

Ma Loko o ke Aniani Kū a me ka Mea i Loa'a iā 'Āleka ma Laila, *Looking-Glass* in Hawaiian, tr. R. Keao NeSmith, 2012

Aliz kalandjai Csodaországban,
Alice in Hungarian, tr. Anikó Szilágyi, 2013

Eachtra Eibhlíse i dTír na nIontas,
Alice in Irish, tr. Pádraig Ó Cadhla (1922), 2015

Eachtraí Eilíse i dTír na nIontas, *Alice* in Irish, tr. Nicholas Williams, 2007

Lastall den Scáthán agus a bhFuair Eilís Ann Roimpi,
Looking-Glass in Irish, tr. Nicholas Williams, 2009

Le Avventure di Alice nel Paese delle Meraviglie,
Alice in Italian, tr. Teodorico Pietrocòla Rossetti, 2010

Alis Advencha ina Wandalan,
Alice in Jamaican Creole, tr. Tamirand Nnena De Lisser, 2016

L's Aventuthes d'Alice en Êmèrvil'lie,
Alice in Jèrriais, tr. Geraint Williams, 2012

L'Travèrs du Mitheux et chein qu'Alice y dêmuchit,
Looking-Glass in Jèrriais, tr. Geraint Williams, 2012

Las Aventuras de Alisia en el Paiz de las Maraviyas,
Alice in Ladino, tr. Avner Perez, 2014

Alisis pīdzeivuojumi Breinumu zemē,
Alice in Latgalian, tr. Evika Muizniece, 2015

Alicia in Terra Mirabili, *Alice* in Latin, tr. Clive Harcourt Carruthers, 2011

Aliciae per Speculum Trānsitus (Quaeque Ibi Invēnit),
Looking-Glass in Latin, tr. Clive Harcourt Carruthers, Forthcoming

Alisa-ney Aventuras in Divalanda, *Alice* in Lingua de Planeta (Lidepla), tr. Anastasia Lysenko & Dmitry Ivanov, 2014

La aventuras de Alisia en la pais de mervelias,
Alice in Lingua Franca Nova, tr. Simon Davies, 2012

Alice ẹhr Ẹventüürn in't Wunnerland,
Alice in Low German, tr. Reinhard F. Hahn, 2010

Contoyrtyssyn Ealish ayns Çheer ny Yindyssyn,
Alice in Manx, tr. Brian Stowell, 2010

Ko Ngā Takahanga i a Ārihi i Te Ao Mīharo,
Alice in Māori, tr. Tom Roa, 2015

Dee Erläwnisse von Alice em Wundalaund,
Alice in Mennonite Low German, tr. Jack Thiessen, 2012

Auanturiou adelis en Bro an Marthou,
Alice in Middle Breton, tr. Herve Le Bihan & Herve Kerrain, Forthcoming

The Aventures of Alys in Wondyr Lond,
Alice in Middle English, tr. Brian S. Lee, 2013

L'Avventure d'Alice 'int' 'o Paese d' 'e Maraveglie,
Alice in Neapolitan, tr. Roberto D'Ajello, 2016

L'Aventuros de Alis in Marvoland, *Alice* in Neo, tr. Ralph Midgley, 2013

Ǣðelgȳðe Ellendǣda on Wundorlande,
Alice in Old English, tr. Peter S. Baker, 2015

Alice Contada aos Mais Pequenos,
The Nursery "Alice" in Portuguese, tr., Rogério Miguel Puga, 2015

Соня въ царствѣ дива (Sonia v tsarstvie diva):
Sonja in a Kingdom of Wonder,
Alice in facsimile of the 1879 first Russian translation, 2013

Охота на Снарка (Okhota na Snarka),
The Hunting of the Snark in Russian, tr. Victor Fet, 2016

Ia Aventures as Alice in Daumsenland,
Alice in Sambahsa, tr. Olivier Simon, 2013

ʻO Tāfaoga a ʻĀlise i le Nuʻu o Mea Ofoofogia,
Alice in Samoan, tr. Luafata Simanu-Klutz, 2013

Eachdraidh Ealasaid ann an Tìr nan Iongantas,
Alice in Scottish Gaelic, tr. Moray Watson, 2012

Alice's Adventchers in Wunderland,
Alice in Scouse, tr. Marvin R. Sumner, 2015

Mbalango wa Alice eTikweni ra Swihlamariso,
Alice in Shangani, tr. Peniah Mabaso & Steyn Khesani Madlome, 2015

Ahlice's Aveenturs in Wunderlaant,
Alice in Border Scots, tr. Cameron Halfpenny 2015

Alice's Mishanters in e Land o Farlies,
Alice in Caithness Scots, tr. Catherine Byrne 2014

Alice's Adventirs in Wunnerlaun,
Alice in Glaswegian Scots, tr. Thomas Clark, 2014

Ailice's Anters in Ferlielann,
Alice in North-East Scots (Doric), tr. Derrick McClure, 2012

Alice's Adventirs in Wonderlaand,
Alice in Shetland Scots, tr. Laureen Johnson, 2012

Ailice's Àventurs in Wunnerland,
Alice in Southeast Central Scots, tr. Sandy Fleemin, 2011

Ailis's Anterins i the Laun o Ferlies,
Alice in Synthetic Scots, tr. Andrew McCallum, 2013

Alice's Carrànts in Wunnerlan,
Alice in Ulster Scots, tr. Anne Morrison-Smyth, 2013

Alison's Jants in Ferlieland,
Alice in West-Central Scots, tr. James Andrew Begg, 2014

Alice muNyika yeMashiripiti,
Alice in Shona, tr. Shumirai Nyota & Tsitsi Nyoni, 2015

Alis bu Cëlmo dac Cojube w dat Tantelat,
Alice in Ṣurayt, tr. Jan Beṯ-Ṣawoce, 2015

Alisi Ndani ya Nchi ya Ajabu, *Alice* in Swahili, tr. Ida Hadjuvayanis, 2015

Alices Äventyr i Sagolandet, *Alice* in Swedish, tr. Emily Nonnen, 2010

'Alisi 'i he Fonua 'o e Fakaofo',
Alice in Tongan, tr. Siutāula Cocker & Telesia Kalavite, 2014

Ventürs jiela Lälid in Stunalän, *Alice* in Volapük, tr. Ralph Midgley, 2016

Lès-avirètes da Alice ô payis dès mèrvèyes,
Alice in Walloon, tr. Jean-Luc Fauconnier, 2012

Anturiaethau Alys yng Ngwlad Hud, *Alice* in Welsh, tr. Selyf Roberts, 2010

I Avventur de Alìs ind el Paes di Meravili,
Alice in Western Lombard, tr. GianPietro Gallinelli, 2015

Di Avantures fun Alis in Vunderland,
Alice in Yiddish, tr. Joan Braman, 2015

Alises Avantures in Vunderland,
Alice in Yiddish, tr. Adina Bar-El, Forthcoming

Insumansumane Zika-Alice,
Alice in Zimbabwean Ndebele, tr. Dion Nkomo, 2015

U-Alice Ezweni Lezimanga, *Alice* in Zulu, tr. Bhekinkosi Ntuli, 2014

www.ingramcontent.com/pod-product-compliance
Ingram Content Group UK Ltd.
Pitfield, Milton Keynes, MK11 3LW, UK
UKHW040032200726
13854UKWH00001B/476